Stephen Coulter was born in London, and educated in England and France. He was for several years Chief Correspondent in Paris for the *Sunday Times*, and its Special Correspondent in India, Africa, Russia and Western Europe.

'Confused sounds came from the forward area. At the back of his mind, Lieutenant Bailey heard men shouting. He could feel the distinct sternward tilt of the ship. A smell of burning had drifted into the control room . . .'

'Apart from the tension among the trapped crew there are some disturbing implications here which lift the book right above the ordinary thriller level'
Guardian

Also by Stephen Coulter

Account to Render
The Chateau
Embassy
Stranger Called the Blues
Death in the Sun
The Soyuz Affair

Stephen Coulter

Threshold

PANTHER
GRANADA PUBLISHING
London Toronto Sydney New York

Published by Granada Publishing Limited
in Panther Books 1980

ISBN 0 586 04940 1

First published in Great Britain by
William Heinemann Ltd 1964
Copyright © Stephen Coulter 1964

Granada Publishing Limited
Frogmore, St Albans, Herts AL2 2NF
and
3 Upper James Street, London W1R 4BP
866 United Nations Plaza, New York, NY 10017, USA
117 York Street, Sydney, NSW 2000, Australia
100 Skyway Avenue, Rexdale, Ontario, M9W 3A6, Canada
PO Box 84165, Greenside, 2034 Johannesburg, South Africa
CML Centre, Queen & Wyndham, Auckland 1, New Zealand

Made and printed in Great Britain by
Richard Clay (The Chaucer Press) Ltd
Bungay, Suffolk
Set in Linotype Plantin

Granada ®
Granada Publishing ®

'. . . the pantomime of nuclear independence . . .'

The Times September 11th, 1963

'No sir. It would not be in the public interest for me to comment on these reports.'

The Prime Minister in the House of Commons

CHAPTER ONE

AT 0250 HOURS on June 14th, immediately before the event, the nuclear submarine HMS *Uranus* was proceeding just below periscope depth at 150 feet, making 40 knots. Course was 095. There was no vibration. A faint hum, like the hum of electric wires, permeated the ship. Occasionally the rhythmic racking of the scrubbers purifying the air broke through and then faded again. There were 102 men on board; 9 officers and 93 men.

At 0250 hours, the Commanding Officer, Lieutenant-Commander Clyde Jason, Royal Navy, had reached the deck below the control room and was going towards his cabin. He was thirty-five years old, medium height. There was a small scar on his jaw. He had blue eyes. He was good looking.

Jason entered his cabin, a 7- by 8-foot space with bunk, combined table-drawer-desk unit, wash-basin, clock, handset telephone, fan and safe. The white paintwork was fresh, since the submarine was new. Jason shut the door behind him, took keys from his pocket, bent down and unlocked the safe alongside the bunk. He took out a clip of pink signals: *Uranus* from Ministry of Defence. He flipped back the top two and stood reading the third.

It was 0251 and 30 seconds.

In the control room immediately under the bridge in the ship's fin – the superstructure known on conventional submarines as the conning-tower – the officer of the watch was Lieutenant Bailey. He was twenty-four and looked younger: brown hair, prominent cheek muscles. He was standing behind and between the two ratings seated in parallel steel-framed upholstered seats steering the ship. The two men sat, facing forward, in front of the black panel of dials and indicators forming a bulkhead across the compartment. Each held a steering-wheel, shaped like an aircraft-type joystick with a semicircular grip handle. The man on the port side was watching an illuminated compass. He was steering the course. The other man had his eyes on the circular dial in front of him. The dial gave the ship's angle and trim. This man's wheel controlled the hydroplanes.

Lieutenant Bailey watched the needle of the dial. He said, 'Take some of that angle off, Lockwood.'

'Angle off, sir.' The rating eased the wheel back like a joystick. The needle of the dial swung fractionally.

Lieutenant Bailey turned away. His glance took in the three ratings, two with earphones, at the switchboard on the starboard side. The switchboard, dull black metal, rose the full height of the compartment and carried eighteen illuminated dials, twelve gauges; indicators, a number of switches, two telephone hand-sets and three speaking-tubes. This switchboard operated, among other things, ballast tanks, periscopes, some of the intercom, one section of the air pumps and one of the air-purifying systems. Chief Petty Officer Fivesman, who was on watch with Lieutenant Bailey, was tying a fancy knot on a telescope.

Lieutenant Bailey took five paces across the control room and into the short alleyway leading aft to the navigation room for exercise. One hour before, the ship had made a sharp alteration in course. Lieutenant Bailey did not know why. There was nothing on his mind.

The time was 0254 hours.

The remaining officers and men were distributed throughout the ship. Lieutenant Connor, the First Lieutenant, was walking along the cat-walk past the reactor compartment. He headed towards the alleyway between the missile racks, eight on each side, making for the control room. Behind him, at a glass panel giving into the reactor room itself, a rating sat in a bucket seat facing dials and gauges. He was monitoring temperatures, pressures, and the flow of liquid sodium transmitting the heat of the fissioning uranium in the submarine's reactor. At a panel farther forward another man faced a bank of controls and from time to time turned a synchronization crank.

8

Thirty men were off watch. All but four were asleep in the crew's quarters two decks below the control room. The four lay on their bunks reading and smoking. The pervasive whine from the turbines seemed slightly louder here.

There were three men in the torpedo room at the ship's nose. One of them was a visitor from aft. On the deck beneath these, two ratings with earphones were seated in the sonar room. The ping-ping of the sonar impulses sounded regularly. Every few seconds the men glanced at the sonar screens.

One man of the engine-room watch had just left the steam condenser to go to the heads. Otherwise the engine-room watch was complete. In the galley a cook was preparing a snack to be left out for the watch coming off duty. Deep in the lowest bay of the ship two ratings were standing talking alongside the missile guidance computers in the big safe. The computers were not working.

At 0255 there was an explosion. It came from a small compartment near the main gyro room at the bottom of the ship. It was followed immediately by what seemed to be a second explosion. This was farther aft, near the nuclear reactor.

The ship shook violently. There were crashes as things fell and a bell, set off inadvertently, started ringing. The lights went out in different compartments but remained on in the control room.

Lieutenant Bailey was thrown against one of the twin periscope columns, both lowered. He saved himself from falling.

'What the hell?'

The ship lurched and rolled to port. Grabbing support, Bailey stepped up behind the two steersmen. The man on the hydroplanes was depressing and turning his wheel, trying to steady the moving needle in the dial. Bailey said urgently, 'Pull the stern up, Lockwood.'

'Aye, aye, sir.'

'One hundred and sixty-five feet, sir,' Chief Petty Officer Fivesman said.

'What?' Bailey looked up at the main depth gauge.

'Ship's gaining depth, sir.'

Bailey turned to the switchboard. 'Captain to control room.'

9

'Captain to control room, sir,' the rating said. He threw a switch, speaking into a mike. 'Captain to control room. Captain to control room, sir.'

'One hundred and eighty feet. Still increasing depth, sir.'

Confused sounds came from the forward area. At the back of his mind, Lieutenant Bailey heard men shouting. He could feel the distinct sternward tilt of the ship. A smell of burning had drifted into the control room.

'Where's Number One?'

Fivesman didn't answer. He snatched a buzzing telephone.

'Engine room reports flooding, sir. Explosion just for'ard, probably in the reactor compartment.'

'We've lost way, sir. Speed fifteen knots and falling.'

A rating had appeared from the navigation room. 'Damage near the missiles, sir. Water coming in fast.'

'Get back to your station!'

'After planes won't answer, sir,' said the steersman.

'Switch to emergency lighting,' Bailey said.

'One hundred and ninety feet, sir,' Fivesman said. Bailey's eyes went back to the depth gauge. The needle was slowly moving round. Bailey and Fivesman exchanged a look.

'Stand by to surface.'

Fivesman repeated the order.

'Shut main vents.'

'Shut main vents, sir.' Fivesman turned to the switchboard to see the order carried out. 'All main vents shut, sir.'

Bailey said, 'Blow all main ballast.'

'Blow all main ballast, sir,' the switchboard said. Both nearer switchboard men moved levers and there was the hissing of air into the tanks.

'Here's the Captain, sir.'

Jason and Lieutenant Connor burst into the control room at the same moment. Jason had a small cut over one eye where the explosion had pitched him forward into a bulkhead fitting. He threw down an armful of cipher books from the safe.

'What's wrong?'

'Blowing main ballast, sir. There's been —'

Jason cut in, 'Cancel that order. Stop blowing.'

'We're flooding, sir. Hydroplanes don't answer,' Bailey said.

'I said cancel it!'

'Stop blowing. Stop blowing.'

'But —' Connor began, then stopped. He looked intently at Jason. Connor's face and uniform were smudged with oil. He had been knocked over. Then he looked at the depth gauge.

'What happened?' Jason said.

'Engine room reports an explosion probably from the reactor compartment. It's flooding.'

'There was another explosion below. Or it seemed like it.'

They were all holding on. The ship was lurching to port. The steersman was trying to keep trim as the water entered and men in other parts of the ship moved about.

'Water flooding the galley, sir. Several men dead.'

'That was why I ordered the main ballast blown, sir,' Bailey said.

Jason said nothing. The powerful gushing of water also came from beyond the navigating room. They all looked at the depth gauge. The brief silence seemed to Connor intolerable.

'After plane not answering, sir.'

'Engine room reports main turbine stopped, sir. Auxiliary seems intact.'

'Speed?' Jason said.

'Three knots, sir.'

'Two hundred and ten feet, sir,' Fivesman said.

'We are sinking without control, sir,' Connor said. 'We'll never get up unless we try now.'

'Shut watertight doors,' Jason cut the words off. He was standing apart from the rest. He had his tunic on over a white roll-collar jersey. He needed a shave. He was watching the depth gauge.

'Two hundred and twenty-five feet, sir,' Fivesman said.

'Flooding in crew's quarters, sir. Men dead.'

Men had crowded into the control room, coming up the ladder from below. Two moved over and shut the watertight hatch over the ladder. The door leading from the control room to the navigating room immediately aft was already shut.

'Two hundred and thirty-five feet, sir.'

11

'We must blow the tanks, sir. For God's sake,' Connor said.

Jason stood looking at the depth gauge. Except for the steersmen, the others were behind him.

'What's the matter, sir?' Connor stepped forward. There was great tension in his face. Jason did not move. Then he said, 'Surface. Blow all main ballast.'

There was a sound like a gasp from those behind him.

'Blow all main tanks,' the switchboard eagerly repeated. The air began to whistle again.

Jason had not moved. They were all listening to the sound of the blow-up and watching the depth gauge. Fivesman stopped announcing. The needle continued to move round. Oil was running down the deck.

Two hundred and forty-five feet.

'Main tanks blown, sir.'

'Blow internal tanks,' Jason said.

'Blow internal tanks, sir.'

The air-filled tanks were having no effect. It meant that one or several main compartments were flooded. The submarine was sinking, well down by the stern.

'Full ahead together,' Jason said.

Two hundred and fifty-five feet.

Two hundred and seventy feet.

There was a bump. Then several lesser ones. Everything shook. Glass broke somewhere and fell tinkling. The deck had evened out. The submarine lurched slowly back from the port side. The hum had stopped. There was nothing but the faint uneven sound of the scrubber and the quiet breathing of the men. It was 0259 hours.

HMS *Uranus* was resting on the bottom.

Lieutenant-Commander Jason turned to the switchboard. 'The watertight door situation has not been reported.'

The nearest switchboard operator looked over his shoulder. 'I can't get the missile control room, sir. Or the crew's quarters.'

'Gyro room isn't answering, sir,' the second operator said.

Jason went to the intercom, unhooked the telephone and

rang the main engine room. He stood waiting for about twenty seconds. There was no reply. He rang the engine-room compartment above the main one. Somebody said, 'Hello?'

'Captain speaking,' Jason said. 'Give me the officer of the watch.'

There was a pause, a slightly confused tangle of voices speaking near the mouthpiece at the other end. Then another voice answered, 'No officers here, sir.'

'What's your situation?'

'We're all right, sir. Watertight doors shut. Compartment below flooded.' The voice was quiet but edged with tension.

'Stand by the intercom,' Jason said and rang off.

He buzzed the two small after engine-room compartments. Neither answered. Nevertheless, in the sternmost of these compartments, a Mechanical Engineer rating was speaking urgently into the intercom. 'Hello... hello... This is ME Beale. Hello . . . After engine-room compartment. ME Beale . . .' The intercom was out of commission just forward and Beale's voice was inaudible beyond the steel bulkhead of the compartment.

From the switchboard panel, Lieutenant Connor said: 'Watertight doors 1 and 3 shut, sir; they're control room to navigation room; number 6 shut, sir, aft of crew's mess. Number 11B shut, by the galley. Numbers 24 and 26 shut, they're after engine-room compartments C1 and C2. Also 28A and 26H, that's the watertight hatch in C2. All the others indicate still open, sir.' Lieutenant Connor was reading from the rows of buttons on the switchboard panel which lit red when the watertight doors were shut. Eight buttons were lit.

Lieutenant-Commander Jason stood still holding the intercom telephone at the end of its wire. The wire extended in coils like a spring. He hung up and took the microphone of the Tannoy, the general broadcasting system, and switched on. Now his voice would go to all parts of the ship simultaneously. There were similar mikes in several of the ship's compartments, so that exchanges could be made over this system as well as over the ordinary intercom telephone.

'Captain speaking. Captain speaking. Officers will report

13

the situation according to the emergency plan in their compartment. Emergency Section One; what is your situation? Emergency Section One please, that is Torpedoes. What is your situation?'

There were mike taps and noises. A voice said muzzily, 'Petty Officer Fitch speaking, sir. Torpedo compartment and crew's mess in order, sir. Watertight door to crew's quarters shut, sir, because flooding on the other side. We're on emergency lighting. Don't look like any other damage.'

'Lieutenant Bailey is here with us in the control room,' Jason said. 'There is no officer with you?'

'No, sir.'

'Are you making water?'

'No, sir.'

'How many of you are there?'

A pause. 'Seven – no, eight, sir.'

'Very well. Emergency Section Two.'

'That's wardroom and control room, both intact, sir,' Connor said. The wardroom adjoined the control room on the same deck.

'Emergency Section Three,' Jason said into the mike. 'That is Galley and Compartment A2. How are you placed?' No reply. Jason's eyes went down the row of switches while he waited. He repeated, 'Captain speaking. Can you hear me, galley? What is your situation?' There was no answer. 'Emergency Section Four. Crew's quarters and Compartment E5. What is the situation with you?' No answer. The control-room clock seemed to have a loud tick. 'Computer compartment?' In the same steady, unhurried voice, Jason went through one after the other. There was no answer from the missile compartment, the missile control room, the main gyro room, storeroom, computer compartment, or the smaller compartments on the lowest deck of the submarine. The nucleonics room amidships, next to the missile control room, did not answer, nor did the navigation room immediately aft of the control room, nor the radio cubicle.

'Emergency Section Fourteen, engine-room generating compartment. How do you stand, please?' No reply there

14

either. At the next section, the reply came through on the ordinary intercom telephone. The voice at the other end said, 'Petty Officer Punchard speaking, sir. There's six of us in here, sir. Everything tickety-boo. One man hurt, that's all. But he'll be all right. The rest of the engine room seems to be out of commission. What happened, sir? Some of 'em saw a bloody great – a flash, sir, from the reactor compartment and we —'

'Thanks, Punchard. After engine-room compartments C1 and C2 report your situation.' No answer. 'Captain speaking: hello compartments C1 and C2. We know your watertight doors are shut. Can't you hear me? Hello? . . . hello?'

Jason's eyes met Connor's. 'There must be somebody down there if the doors are shut.' He lifted the mike again. Slowly, with pauses between the names, he said, 'Lieutenant Harvey? Captain calling Lieutenant Harvey, Lieutenant Ballard? Lieutenant Pinkney? Lieutenant Piper? Sub-Lieutenant Wade? Wade, can you hear me? Sub-Lieutenant Rumbold?' There were no responses.

Lieutenant-Commander Jason handed the mike to Connor. His gesture was a shade brisker than usual. 'Check each compartment again.'

He crossed to the other side of the control room and picked up the bag in which he had placed the clip of signals. The bag was fitted with a bar of lead, sewn into the bottom, and perforated with brass-rimmed holes. 'Lieutenant Bailey, take those cipher books to the bridge.'

'Yes, sir.'

Bailey gathered up the books from where Jason had dumped them. They were in lead-weighted jackets. He climbed up the ladder into the fin. The small bridge with its windscreen-shaped porthole, voice-pipes, chart table, intercom mike and telephone, was a compartment on its own situated halfway up the fin and used when navigating on the surface. Above it was the upper bridge compartment where officers could stand, on the surface, with head and shoulders in the open. Both the bridge and this upper compartment were traversed by the columns of the twin periscopes and, just aft, the mast carrying

15

the radar and schnorkel. The fin was fitted to serve as an escape chamber. There were two other escape chambers in the submarine – one aft, in the engine room, and the other forward in the torpedo compartment.

Jason waited for Connor to finish. The emergency light close overhead threw deep shadows on his face, accentuating the good looks. In Jason's quietness, there was now something colder.

Connor stopped speaking and racked up the mike. 'That's all, sir.' For the first time, Jason turned and looked at the men crowded into the rear of the control room. One was lying on the deck, propped against a control console. They were all silent and still. They stood in a tableau. Two or three still had their hats on the back of their heads, some were in dungarees or overalls or undervests. One man was wearing only his underpants and socks. Connor had fallen out the two steersmen who had joined the rest.

Jason's eyes went over their faces; Chief Petty Officer Fivesman, a solemn face like a stage butler's with a great slit mouth; Chief Petty Officer Doggart, pudgy, curls on his forehead; Leading Radio Operator Kirby, short and curly-haired too; Leading Seaman (Radar Plot) Evans, pale, intense and sandy, and the rest. He looked at all of them and they returned his look as if they were transmitting faith to him. He received the silent communication. He said to the man on the deck, 'What's the trouble, Trimmer?'

The man stirred painfully, looked up. 'Nothing much, sir. Me legs, sir.'

'How many here?' Jason said to Connor.

'Twelve.' With the three officers, that made fifteen.

'We'll take a roll-call.' Jason went to the intercom telephone and rang the torpedo compartment. 'Take down the names as I give them, Lieutenant Bailey.'

'Hello? Torpedoes.'

'Petty Officer Fitch? Captain speaking. Give me your names.'

In the torpedo compartment, Petty Officer Fitch, naked to the waist, looked over his shoulder at the three men he could

16

see in the spaces by the tubes. Others were out of sight in the mess beyond.

'Petty Officer Robertson, sir. Leading ME Bosco ... Leading ME Cubit ... Robbie, who's the others? Wait a minute, sir ...'

When he had all eight names, Jason rang the engine room and took the names of the six there. Then he stepped over to a sectional drawing of *Uranus* fixed to the bulkhead aft of the switchboard panel. The drawing was covered with plexiglass. When Jason tried to block off the waterlogged sections with hatching, the ink would not take. Connor produced a soft-nosed red pencil and they outlined the compartments still intact. These were the fin – that is, the whole superstructure leading down to the control room; the wardroom, four times the size of an ordinary submarine's wardroom, forward of and adjoining the control room; and the control room itself. In this section there were the Captain, Lieutenant Connor the No. 1, Lieutenant Bailey (Torpedo Officer), Chief Petty Officer Fivesman (Coxswain), Chief Petty Officer Doggart (Chief Radio Electrical Artificer), Leading Radio Operator Kirby, Leading Electrical Mechanic MacFall, Electrical Mechanics Farrell and Groves, Leading Seamen (Radar Plot) Evans and Trimmer, Leading Stores Assistant Hoyle, Leading Seaman Lockwood, Leading Writer Monkhouse and Ordnance Artificer Wisden.

On the deck below this and forward of it, the torpedo compartment and the adjoining crew's mess were also intact. In them were: Petty Officer Electrical Artificer Fitch, Petty Officer Ordnance Artificer Robertson, Leading Mechanical Engineers Cubit and Bosco, Leading Seaman (Torpedo Anti-Submarine) Haynes, Able Seaman Gunner Wingrove, Sick Berth Attendant Green and Ordinary Steward Savage.

The six in the engine room were: Petty Officer Mechanical Engineer Punchard, Leading Engine Room Artificer Maxwell, Leading Mechanical Engineer Vickers, Mechanical Engineers Tippett, Acre and Davis.

Finally, unknown to the rest of the ship and therefore not in Jason's count, were two men in the two small after engine-

17

room compartments. They were Petty Officer Mechanician Grimble and Mechanical Engineer Beale. The rest of *Uranus*'s crew were dead. The submarine was disabled.

Jason and Connor went over to the main control panel. Jason called Chief Petty Officer Doggart over, but didn't say anything to him immediately. Doggart, the unfailing extrovert, was foil and complement to Fivesman who was saturnine and a bit of the old retainer. Jason stood looking over the dials and gauges of the panel.

Many of the needles lay back at zero. Others twitched or flickered feebly, a dial glowed here and there – the nerveresponses, like the twitchings of a corpse, still coming from some parts of the ship. The operators were throwing switches here and there, testing, trying to recover a contact, to cajole a stronger gleam.

'What scrubber is this working?' Jason asked.

'The one in A3, I think, sir,' the operator said. 'They are both on this same connection.'

'Chief, which is it?'

Doggart followed a set of feed-in cables to a point among a mass of others on the bulkhead. He unshipped an inspection plate and worked inside for several minutes. 'It's A3, sir. That's the smaller one by the galley. There's a watertight door which shuts itself on a cell when the main scrubber cuts off without control, sir.'

'That's true, I forgot, sir. It accounts for one of those doors,' Connor said.

Jason nodded. He was listening to the irregular throb coming from the scrubber vent above. The scrubbers were the machines which rid the submarine of carbon dioxide. They sucked in the air exhaled by the crew, bathed it in an absorbent liquid, boiled it and pumped out the CO_2. The system then bled in more oxygen and redistributed the reconditioned air through the ship.

The rhythm and noise of the scrubbers varied. Near to, they often made a terrible racket. But sometimes they were quiet. The machines seemed to be stealthy, to be breathing softly and watching the men. When this happened, sleeping men woke up. They lay in their bunks listening for the machines' breathing. It was as if they thought the machines were surreptitiously leaving them, somehow withdrawing from this deadly steel tube under the ocean and leaving them to die. Men got up and stood with their heads turned upwards to the vents. At other times, the scrubbers kept wavering and hesitating, until somebody would make a quick move away so as not to tell the things to shut up – maybe yell at them. The scrubbers hardly ever seemed to be friendly. They seemed to be jokes on the men. They seemed to be saying that they were going to take it out on them when they had the chance.

Jason said, 'Have you checked radiation, Lieutenant Bailey?'

Connor was busy organizing the men into tasks and getting Trimmer, the injured man, attended to. The tableau had broken up. The control room was full of activity. Men passed into the wardroom beyond.

Jason bent at the panel going over the controls. He left it, crossed to another console and checked there. There were three square green panes behind which liquid floated and a scale marked off in steel wire. Jason turned the adjuster dials. There was no change in the green panes. The reactor was certainly flooded. There was heavy protective shielding against radiation for crew and machinery. During his eight months course before he had taken command, Jason had been told that *Uranus* would never get more than about 200 milliroentgens a year. Any industrial firm had far more than that. The permitted dose of radiation in industry was 300 milliroentgens a week. But if an explosion had occurred in the reactor compartment itself? The training course had not gone seriously into that.

Connor had sent Kirby, the radio operator, to the emergency receiver housed in a cubicle behind the control room.

'How are we off for water?' Jason said.

Connor said, 'There's a tap in the wardrobe pantry. The others ought to be all right. I'll see.' He turned away to the intercom with an unusual movement. Jason caught the un-

19

certainty on Connor's face and a flash of resentment.

Kirby came back and reported that the emergency radio receiver was working. Kirby was wiry and imperturbable. He had a broad Scots accent. Jason said, 'Have you got anybody to keep watch with you, Kirby?'

'Aye, aye, sir, Groves. He's been on the radio course, sir.'

'All right. Chief, tell off Groves to share radio watch with Leading RO Kirby.'

'Yes, sir.' Chief Petty Officer Fivesman hesitated, turned back. 'Whereabouts are we, sir?'

That was unusual too. Jason thought they were a bloody good lot to keep their apprehension down to such small signs. 'Must be on the bottom, Chief, I think,' he said gently.

'Aye, aye, sir.' Fivesman turned to carry out the order.

Lieutenant Connor hung up the intercom telephone and came over. 'The party for'ard has water in the crew mess. There's a lead-in there from the galley. The engine room say they can tap the steam-condenser supply.' He was looking at Jason narrowly.

'All right,' Jason said. He went to the Tannoy and unhooked the mike. He spoke firmly and evenly. 'This is the Captain speaking to ship's company. Captain speaking to all of you. We've had some sort of mishap. I don't know what it was and we don't look like finding out in a hurry. We're on the bottom, out of commission and can't surface. We have lost shipmates but there are a lot of us alive and with a bit of luck we ought to get through. The scrubber, as you can hear, is working. Don't smoke more than you can help because cigarettes help to build up CO_2. There's no radiation danger. (Jason did not look at Bailey.) As you know, the firebox of the reactor is so built that it's harmless even if it is swamped. Our radio receiver is working. So altogether we aren't badly off. Any of you can call me on intercom if there are material changes in your compartment. Otherwise, don't use it more than you need because of the battery. That goes for lights too. Make yourselves as comfortable as you can. Maybe we won't have to wait long. That's all.'

He hung up the mike quickly. He didn't want any questions.

He felt Connor's close look, sensed Connor's puzzlement at the things he had not said. Bailey was standing by with a rating in dungarees holding a metal box with wired tube attachment – the geiger counter. 'Nothing more than usual, sir,' Bailey said.

Jason nodded. He picked up the leaded bag, looked round. Two ratings were at the control panel. A group of others were at the back of the control room. Jason swung himself on to the ladder leading up into the superstructure and climbed up to the bridge.

Connor watched Jason's feet disappear. He felt anger, uncertainty carrying him into a dark zone where the safe references of duty and command vanished. It made Connor afraid. He forced himself to say, 'Chief, you'd better check the emergency lighting.'

'Aye, aye, sir,' Doggart said.

Connor was also sharply aware of the silence of the ship. A nuclear submarine is quiet. But now *Uranus* had reached a degree of quietness that Connor had never known. It was quieter even than when they were creeping after some sonar target – he noticed that the scrubber was scarcely whispering in its secret voice – when everybody moved softly about the ship and spoke in low tones. He could hear the men behind him and the occasional sounds from the wardroom. But they were muffled, as if the men had the same feeling. But it was the machinery, of course, that you missed, the complex accumulation of sound that you hardly listened to consciously.

He jerked his head to Bailey to indicate that he was going to the bridge, grasped the ladder and climbed up. Jason was at the chart table writing up the log. He was smoking a cigarette. The clip of signals was on the glass-topped chart table, face down. Connor saw the wincing retraction of muscle at the outer corner of Jason's eye which occurred in Jason's bad moments. Jason glanced up but continued writing.

The fear which had appeared in Connor when Jason had been standing in the control room after the explosions was now being momentarily displaced by his anger. Jason went on writing. Connor stood there for a minute; then he couldn't help saying, 'Are you putting in why you didn't blow sooner?'

21

'Yes, I am,' Jason said coldly. He wrote two or three more words, put the pen down. He looked at Connor.

Connor said, 'We might have got up. There was a chance, wasn't there?'

Jason's eye was wincing. He saw the embarrassment behind Connor's anger. 'I don't think I should have blown as it was.'

'What? Do you mean to say —'

Jason said, 'We had orders not to surface.'

'Not to? But good God, it was a crash or something – an emergency.'

'That was why I disregarded the orders. Wrongly. It's in the log.'

Connor looked at him.

'I've put the explosions at about 0255 hours. Right?'

'I – I didn't take a timing.' Connor was completely at a loss.

Jason pushed over his packet of cigarettes. Connor didn't move. Jason said, 'Besides the signal you saw when we sailed, we had a sealed order. I didn't tell you. I wasn't expected to. The day before yesterday, I was told to open it and proceed when I had a further signal which we received an hour and a half ago. You were off watch.'

'When we altered course and went to full ahead?'

Jason nodded.

'Where does that put us now, then?' Connor said.

'About seven miles inside Russian territorial waters.'

THERE WAS a pause. Connor said, 'God Almighty.' He was still readjusting to the disappearance of his fear about Jason, to the return to the real world he understood and loved.

Jason picked up the signal clip. 'This says that I am only to tell the navigating officer of the course. I am to communicate the orders to my Number One "as late as practical" and then not more of them than is necessary for general purposes. Nobody else is to be informed. Now you know where we are, it is obvious why.'

This also explained the unusual routine of the last forty-eight hours – Jason and the navigator plotting the course alone, taking sights with the periscope sextant on their own and working out the position in Jason's cabin instead of in the navigating room, Jason writing up a separate copy of the log.

Connor wanted to express his regret and shame at thinking that Jason had fallen short of his duty. He knew that he would never be able to express the enormity of his relief. He said, 'I made a damned silly mistake, sir —'

'You ought to see the orders now, at any rate. I'm disobeying My Lords Commissioners – I should say the Ministry – again.' Jason's brow wrinkled and he gave a half-melancholy grin. He flipped back the top two signals and handed over the clip.

Top Secret Personal to Commanding Officer For Your Eyes Only [Connor read at the top of the signal].

From position 17' 00" E 72' 11" N, you will proceed submerged at all possible speed on exact course given in following signal A 150 MD16 so as to make landfall by periscope on the Soviet coast at approximately 0300 hours 14 June at position 44' 36" E 67' 10" N. The operation will oblige you to enter Soviet territorial waters. At first light or as soon after as visibility permits you will take periscope photographs of shore installations at Chizha in particular the three towers situated on a bearing 330 from end of breakwater. The exact time at which these photographs are taken must be noted (not in ship's log, see Chief of Naval Staff's ASA 1906/U5). When photographs have been obtained, you will submerge for one hour, return to periscope depth and again photograph the installations, taking particular care to cover the three towers. Any unusual activity ashore should be noted and timed exactly. It is important that second series of photographs be obtained as exactly as possible one hour after first. When these have been procured you will submerge and withdraw at all possible speed through positions given in A 150 MD16 Part Two.

There followed further instructions for signalling once well back in international waters, the wavelengths on which the Ministry of Defence would be keeping radio watch and the disposal of cipher books during the operation. The orders concluded:

Operation is to be carried out with maximum dispatch. You should spend least possible time in Soviet waters. In the event of any Soviet counter-action or if you suspect you are detected, you will instantly break off operations, submerge to maximum depth, take evasive action and withdraw at all possible speed. Any Soviet fire or depth charging is not repeat not to be answered. The object of the operation is a very fast dash into Soviet waters to obtain data of highest importance. You will not repeat not brief officers or ship's company on your mission. You should give ship's company to understand that you are on routine testing and training exercise.

Connor looked up into Jason's hard grey eyes. The formal phrases of the signal, the word 'Soviet', had produced a subsidiary shock in him. The only sign in Jason was the slight nervous flicking of the muscle at the corner of his eye.

'What were those explosions?' Connor said. 'Are we in a minefield or something?'

'I don't know. They had nothing marked in London. According to the latest Qs there's nothing here.'

'A torpedo?'

Jason shook his head. 'No. Might be underwater defences but there weren't supposed to be any of those either. They were positive about that; and Bailey says he got nothing from the sonar.'

Connor said, 'What are the emergency orders?'

Jason drew on his cigarette, exhaled the smoke, stubbed out the butt. 'I opened the orders you've seen. That's all they contain.'

Connor looked at him, trying to keep the incredulity out of his face.

The six men on the upper deck of the engine room had a good area of space but it was encumbered by machinery. On the other hand, the emergency lighting was bright and the ladder of the after escape chamber descended in the middle of the compartment.

Most of the six happened to be cheerful-spirited men who took adversity well. They had a temperamental capacity for dealing with situations of this sort, which was why they were in the submarine service. They were all modestly off. None of them could expect more than life in a terrace house, the television, a child or two and perhaps a job as a commissionaire when he retired. They felt well-disposed towards the service. But they weren't fiercely devoted to it or dedicated men. They saw vaguely that they would feel stronger towards it after many years in it because it had occupied so much of their lives. But while these years were still passing largely in routine, they were often bored and sometimes cursed the service and wished they were out of it. Otherwise, for much of the time, the Navy was a set of fairly agreeable habits.

They weren't in the least heroic. Life never appeared to them in heroic terms and the men they had known or heard about who had been decorated for what was called heroism were, to them, simply ordinary men who had found themselves in the path of some event or some impulse. It might, they

25

supposed, happen to anybody. They hadn't the imagination to inflate things. Life was composed of commonplace events. If there was a heroic aspect to these men's lives, it was in their humble decency and their cheerfulness.

In the minutes after Jason had finished speaking over the Tannoy, Petty Officer Punchard had begun organizing the six men, allotting each of them an area, verifying the escape gear racked in the compartment. They all understood that there was to be no spoken reference to the moments of their escape or to those killed.

Punchard had a pale washed-out face and thick black hair glistening with brilliantine, done in a quiff. The contrast between the blackness of his hair and the extinction of his face made people think he was ill. But Punchard had a body of steel. He needed three hours' sleep a night. Since his early days in the service, he had been called on for emergency repairs, since he could stay at work on a piece of machinery for days, while others were dropping out for rest or fresh air.

'I suppose they got a crash signal away, Punch?' ME Tippett asked.

'Bet your life.'

'Where are we, Bert?' Vickers said.

'How do I know? Somewhere in the North Atlantic, the Old Man said when we sailed, didn't he?'

' "Exercises in the North Atlantic" was what he said.'

'That was days ago,' ME Davis said. 'You can cross the Atlantic and back in a week in this job.'

'Give us a fag, Bert.'

'You better ration them fags.'

'How about nipping along to the canteen and getting us a tin of Gold Flake, Vick?'

'We ain't going to be here that long.'

'What the 'ell did we hit, Punch?'

'I dunno. Maybe another ship.'

'No. It went off.'

'Vickers and Maxwell, you can unship that guard. Give us a bit more room.'

'Look, Punch, if we straighten out the guard, we can sling it

26

across here and make a bunk.'

'That's it. Go on then.'

ME Acre, with an arm and ribs broken, was sitting with his back against the steam condenser. His breathing was evidently painful.

Davis said, 'Punch, d'you think the water's radioactive and when we get out we're going to get burned up, you know, like them Jap fishermen?'

'You heard what the Captain said. There can't be any danger from the reactor, even if it's flooded.'

'Well, Bob's your uncle.' Tippett held up a packet of cigarettes from a pair of overalls he had found in the compartment.

'Come to think of it, speaking of celebrations,' Punchard said, crossing the compartment, 'I know where somebody used to save his tot.' He bent down and put his hand into an area behind a complex of valves and insulated pipes. He searched round for a moment, then a smile broadened on his face. The others watched him. Slowly he extracted an enamel tea-mug. It was half-full of rum.

'Well now, me old cocks, spirits up!'

The situation of the eight men sharing the torpedo compartment and the crew's mess was a great deal easier. There was space for a man alongside each of the double-banked pairs of tubes. These spaces were the action stations where, in attack, the men would stand facing aft with hands on the firing levers watching the torpedo officer and waiting for his signal to launch the self-homing torpedoes.

The tubes themselves with their unbelievable tangle of copper and steel tubes, gauges, levers, caps, locks, valves, cocks and bars, were burnished and glistening. Deep copper gleams shone from them in the subdued light as the men moved about. On each torpedo tube hung a shining steel plate with the words NOT LOADED. The headroom above the tubes was largely filled with cables and cased connections. In the deckhead over the port tubes was the forward escape chamber. There was room enough on the deck aft of the tubes for another man to lie down.

27

But above all, the eight had the entire crew mess which at meal-times could accommodate thirty-two men and was fitted with benches, three central tables, flaps that pulled down from the bulkhead, a clock, tiny pantry, a shelf of books, set of dominoes and cards. There was also a built-in hi-fi record-player which was not working. The space was designed with clean clear lines and was relatively free of exposed pipes.

In spite of this large comfortable area, the eight men did not show the cheerful extroversion of those in the engine room. The disaster had shaken them all. A large number of the men lost had been killed or drowned near the mess. Four of the eight slouched at one of the mess tables, a couple more were lounging on the far side by the record-player, another moved aimlessly round the compartment. The eighth, Petty Officer Robertson, was apart from the rest, leaning against a tube in the torpedo compartment trying to get a last draw from an eighth of an inch of brown cigarette stub which was burning his lips and fingers. He was also trying to forget the screams, shouts and cries for help he had heard from the men in the condemned areas of the ship as he had shut the watertight doors. It was in the minutes after the tension that it hit you.

He could hear Petty Officer Fitch talking in the mess. Fitch had crinkly ginger hair and a hairless chin and a long pale neck with freckles on it. Leading ME Bosco was Fitch's pal. Robertson conceded that they were two of the most efficient men in the ship. But he disliked them both. He didn't like Leading ME Cubit much better – or Haynes. You didn't know what to make of Leading Seaman Haynes; he was clever. Wingrove was a good man – big and immensely strong. Robertson was thankful for Wingrove. The remaining pair, Savage and Green, were all right, but they would be easily influenced by the others and Savage's nerve was not good.

Robertson trod out the fragment of cigarette on the plating and out of habit picked it up. It wasn't much luck to land up with this lot, he thought. With the experience of an old Navy hand, he knew that there was a latent bloody-mindedness in three or four of the group. For a long time after the Captain had spoken, they had been quiet, uneasy and brooding. To occupy himself, Robertson had tried to get them out of it. But he had been unsuccessful. Fitch and Bosco had lost their usual bounce. Now they were getting it back, talking in the mess.

'I told you there was a Jonah on board this ship,' Bosco said.

'*You* did? You're the bloody Jonah, Bosco. Whyn't you overstay your leave this time?'

'There's been something wrong with the diving planes ever since Portland. What was all that working up for?'

'I tell you I did hear somebody banging at that watertight door when we shut it.'

'Shut up, Savage, will you?' There was silence for a minute.

Green said, 'They took off them three sea valves in dock. I told you, Ginger.'

'If it was a sea valve, it wouldn't have exploded like that,' Fitch said.

'How do you know? If there's a rush of water to the reactor, it's going to go off, ain't it? Stands to reason.'

'You heard what the Old Man said.'

'Christ, that's what they *say*. He's bound to say that.'

Bosco said, 'I know for a fact there was a couple of indicators put on back to front. That dockside fitter told me, you know, Ginge, the little fat one we had a beer with.'

'What indicators?'

'He said when they was shut they showed open.'

'Christ almighty.'

Another silence. The sound of the scrubber faded. They all looked up to the vent. Then the rhythm resumed.

'I tell you I heard —'

'Shut up, Savage, can't you?'

'Why'd we keep taking those dockyard engineers out? It must've been ten trips. There was something wrong on board.'

'What I want to know is why we put on speed,' Leading Seaman Haynes said. He had not spoken before. The others looked at him.

'Perhaps the Old Man knew something was wrong?'

Haynes said, 'Then why not surface? We were going flat out for well over an hour. We haven't done that since the trials. But there was no extra watch on, so they weren't testing anything. I was down aft and they didn't know there either.'

'I reckon it was a collision,' Green said.

There was a chorus of dissent, though none of them could say why they were so sure. Then they began to speculate on the submarine's position. Somebody said, 'Let's ask the Old Man on the blower.'

Nobody moved. 'Go on, Ginger,' Green said. Fitch lit a cigarette, waved out the match, dropped it. They were all waiting for him, but he didn't get up.

Haynes, who was standing, looked down at them contemptuously. 'What's the matter with you?' he said. He crossed to the intercom and rang control room. Jason took the call on the bridge. 'Yes? Captain speaking.'

'Leading Seaman Haynes, torpedo compartment, sir. Men in this section want to know where we are, sir.'

'The orders were, Haynes, to keep these communications down to a minimum. We have to stick to that. Do you understand?'

'Yessir.'

'You all right otherwise?'

'Yessir.'

'Then that's all.' Jason rang off.

Haynes stood motionless for a moment before hooking up the phone. There was a faint flush on his face. But it had gone when he turned. Poorly imitating Jason's voice, he said, 'Keep communications to the minimum. Understand?'

'Well, we can't be in the Atlantic according to the depth gauge,' Fitch said. 'Two hundred and seventy feet.'

'That gauge has been wrong all along,' Cubit said. 'I've seen Harvey trying to adjust it three times.'

'Yes, and the Old Man was down here last week looking at it,' Bosco said. 'We're probably twice that depth.'

In the torpedo room, Robertson took a ball of cotton waste and carefully wiped a spot of oil from the torpedo case. He loved the torpedo mechanism, the gleaming cases, the beautiful and precise complex of steel and copper.

'For Christ's sake, can't we use the escape chamber?'

30

Savage was saying in the mess.

Nobody answered. They seemed to have sunk into their brooding again. Then somebody said, 'What do you reckon you're going to do when you're up there swimming around? Perhaps you can hail the *Queen Mary* as she goes by?'

Another silence.

Robertson heard somebody approaching from the mess and Savage came into the torpedo compartment. Savage stood looking up at the escape chamber. 'Robbie —'

'There's sure to be something on the way out to us now, Savage,' Robertson said. 'They'll have a crash signal away. All we got to do is wait till we get the wire that they're up there ready to pick us up and we can go.'

'How long's it going to be, Robbie?'

'Not long. They can get a couple of big helicopters out, drop a rubber boat. Probably even pick us up with a rope ladder. Matter of hours. You see that programme on the telly the other day? Sea rescue job. Very smart.'

Robertson had a mental picture of the headlines at home. *Nuclear Submarine Disaster. Rescuers dash. 'Good hopes' says Navy*. He could see the consternation in the PO's mess at *Osprey*, the submarine training school at Portland where they had been on courses; there would be whispers and rumours. He shut off thoughts of his wife and six-year-old daughter and Daisy's mother who lived with them in the small Swanage house.

'Come on, Savage, it won't do you any good looking at it.' They went back into the mess. 'Let's get organized, Ginger,' Robertson said.

Fitch looked up. He nodded and all at once was briskly on his feet. With relief, Robertson saw that Fitch's better side was responding. If Fitch wanted, things could go very well indeed.

Collectively with Fitch and Robertson working them as a team, they took stock of their resources. Wingrove's fat geniality also seemed somehow to cheer them up. They searched through the mess, pantry and torpedo compartment. They discovered that activity helped them. As food, they found they had three bars of chocolate, a large tin of baked beans, two tins of sausages and half a stale loaf. There were also some apples, half a pound of canteen gob-stoppers, five packets of cigarettes and six dirty postcards.

As they were deciding on a watch duty – one man to be awake at all times – Savage said, 'Honest, Ginger, what about the reactor? Is it going to go up any minute?'

Fitch said, 'No, it's not.'

Haynes said incisively, 'How do you know?'

Silence. Fitch didn't answer.

'Do you know the conditions in there, Fitch?' Haynes went on. 'Do you know exactly what happened in that reactor room?' Fitch shrugged. 'Because until you do, you can't say if it's not going to blow us all to Jesus – or maybe leak out and give us nuclear nettle-rash. Can you?'

'Ah, stow it.' Wingrove gave a deprecatory laugh but the others took no notice.

Robertson's eyes went round the group. They were all looking at Haynes, except for Fitch. Fitch was looking at his cigarette. Robertson saw that there had been a shift in the relationship. The balance between the men had changed. Haynes was now the leader. Robertson felt uneasy. His eyes went back to Savage. Savage was staring at the bulkhead.

CHAPTER THREE

On the bridge, Jason shut the cipher books and the current tables, put them with the others into the weighted bag. He locked this and put it in the cupboard under the chart table, locking this in turn. He had taken off his jacket and was in the white submariner's sweater. He looked at the thermometer; it was steady at 70. Relative humidity was 53 per cent. He checked the time and wrote the temperature and humidity in the log. Since the disaster Jason had kept the full log himself.

Lieutenant-Commander Jason was the only son of a rich, self-indulgent father who spent hardly any time in England and was a strange figure to Jason and his sister. (Their mother was dead.) Jason had done his national service in the Navy without asking for a deferment and returned to his medical studies. He had a good mind and went through the successive yearly stages with no difficulty. He was attending medical school at a London hospital where he would, if he liked, be able to do post-graduate laboratory work. He had some surgical skill but was drawn to neuropathology and paraplegia. He took a Bachelorship and his LRCP, was preparing his MD and intended trying for a doctorate in surgery later.

The summer before the MD, his father wired for him to come to him in New Delhi where he had fallen ill at the conclusion of some business deal. Jason flew out rather alarmed. His father was up and about when he arrived, treated Jason with his customary flippancy and a week later took a plane to New York. Jason decided to return home by sea. He went to Bombay and booked passage on a ship leaving in two days' time.

He spent the interval wandering about the town which he didn't much care for. He was beckoned to by the Indian whores standing mysteriously silhouetted with their hair down at the dark open windows on the Apollo Bunder. He lunched in the Taj, wincing while an appalling Indian sextet played the airs of an English seaside Palm Lounge ensemble. The arrogant smartness of the British Raj had certainly vanished. He smiled at the Yacht Club, once supremely elegant as described by his father, with its lawns and terrace overlooking the harbour, now displaying a flaking sign: Atomic Energy Commission. He took a train and visited the caves at Kanheri and wandered alone into the empty oppressive temple-rooms in the rocks with their squeaking bats.

He had chosen a ship which carried only thirty passengers. They sailed with nineteen. One of them was Kitty Raikes. She was travelling alone. He found her very attractive. She was eight years older than Jason, with thick fair hair, which had deep ochre gleams in it, and high cheekbones. She had an extraordinary radiance. Any man was aware of her the minute she came into a room or passed by on deck. She dressed with great taste and chic.

Jason spent hours with her. He learned with some surprise, though he didn't know why, that she was married to Victor Raikes, the powerful lawyer. They had a son of eight and a girl of four. She seemed to admire her husband more than love him. When Jason kissed her one night she responded willingly. She was amusing and lighthearted. He spent the night with her in her cabin and knew next day that he was wildly in love with her.

The voyage was rapture, with only a little torment. She told him she had been to India – her family had lived in Delhi, it appeared, and she still had a brother there – after a critical few months with her husband. Raikes was a philanderer. He had humiliated her several times and they had come to the point of divorce. But since she had been away, he had cabled and written to her imploring forgiveness and wanting her back. He had a vast practice, was involved in politics and was at the centre of an influential circle of hard, ambitious men and obviously missed her efficient running of his household.

Was she going back? She didn't know.

Jason found her constantly and wonderfully beautiful. She

was full of wit and intelligence and fascinated him with stories of the world of legal and political power. There was a hardness about this world which shocked him. He couldn't think of her belonging to it. Her husband had a belligerent appetite for power. 'He lives for power,' she said. 'He only has women to break them – throw them aside. He wants me back to keep me watching him do so – power.'

'Then don't go back.'

'Oh,' she said and looked down. 'Not so easy.'

'You don't love him.'

'Darling, give me a cigarette.'

Jason couldn't bring himself to think of the voyage ending. When their train from the docks reached Victoria, the first thing she did was to telephone her husband from a station call-box. She made Jason stand by her while she spoke.

'Can you hear his voice?' She put her hand over the mouth-piece and tilted the receiver. Jason heard Raikes's voice say-ing, 'Do you follow, my dear?' Hastily she put the receiver back to her ear. 'What? I didn't hear.' Finally she finished. 'Doesn't he sound brilliant?' she said to Jason. She was ob-viously happy. This was only early torment.

They took two rooms in a quiet hotel and spent the day together. Jason again asked her to marry him. She kissed him and smiled. At night they made love and Jason went back to his room at dawn. When he woke up at ten and rang her to come to breakfast, the room was empty. She had gone, without leaving a note.

Jason felt at the end of his life. The world was transformed. He only saw ugly, abstracted, indifferent people, people who were hardly alive since they hadn't known her. He only saw her. The memory of her glamour made everything without her shabby and paltry and tasteless.

He didn't know where she had gone. She had said she wasn't going home to Raikes and he couldn't bring himself to telephone, though it was all he thought about. This was the period when he had acquired the wincing of his eye muscle.

Two months later, in misery, he wrote to her at Raikes's London house. She replied and they met. Jason was more in love with her than ever. She was gay and apparently carefree.

They went to the south of France, to a small *auberge* near La Ciotat, and spent ten days there. There was only one other guest in the place, a silent French girl of twenty-three or so recovering from some illness and absorbed in books. They swam in the cold sea and made love, walked, ate bouillabaisse. She responded to his love-making and said a hundred gentle things in these moments.

But when Jason wanted her to fulfil the logic of their situation, to go away together or to marry, she said no. She couldn't. And he saw, from her references, that it was because she did not want to sacrifice her position, her habits, the flattery she got from being in Raikes's power circle. Love between her and Jason meant less to her than the preservation of her mundanity. There was an intense and ravaging community between them in their love-making which sometimes made her weep. Yet she could separate it icily from the rest of her life. It opened no channels into the world she ordinarily lived in.

Jason, a man of feeling, tried to understand this, then to circumvent it. But he couldn't. Back in London, they saw each other fleetingly once or twice and then it ended.

The affair shattered Jason. It ruined his medical studies. He failed his MD. He found his personality had been flawed in a curious way. His capacity for sympathizing with people, for admiring them, let alone loving them, the attributes he most wanted, as a doctor, to keep alive, were diminished. He could not give himself. He could not communicate emotionally at any depth with other people. He could not respond to friendship, sympathy or love. Yet he was aware of this and felt it a terrible loss.

He took some time to find it out. As he gradually discovered it and its effects, he thought of marrying, then saw that this would be fatal. He threw up medicine and managed to get a commission in the Navy. It was still possible then, but he had soon had to weather the blizzard when the Navy was being reduced to nothing by the new defence ideas. Jason took advance courses in new weapons and stayed in the service. He asked for the submarine service. When the nuclear submarines had come along, he had naturally graduated to them. He had recovered all he ever would from the love-affair with Kitty Raikes. But he found that the service offered only limited therapy for his other disability.

Deeply within himself, he struggled to recover from the condition. He kept up with numerous friends and had occasional sad little affairs with girls. He appealed to women and he clung to the feelings of gratitude he had for those he knew. But he remained largely as before. He believed it had arisen from self-defence. He felt himself marooned. There were barriers between him and other people.

None of this appeared on the surface. To his superiors at the Ministry of Defence, Jason was a man of unusually cool and level penetration with an excellent tactical mind and absolutely fair. They rated him highly. Men of this temperament, they knew, often enjoy being uncompromising. Jason used inflexibility in a controlled way, with precision, for exact, limited purposes and without becoming involved personally. The Ministry saw that he was the ideal person for risky assignments. When the Chizha operation was decided on, there was no hesitation in sending Jason in *Uranus*.

Connor came up the ladder as Jason finished the log entry.

'I had them check the battery on the scrubber. It seems all right,' Connor said. 'Do you think we ought to switch the scrubber off for a bit? Work it say twelve hours a day?'

Jason said, 'You can't get a check on the CO_2. We ought to have kept a spare testing set in the control room. Better keep it on.'

'Yes, sir,' Connor said.

Connor had great admiration for Jason. Connor was grandson of Admiral J. G. O'G. Connor, one-time Commander, East Indies Station, and a famous naval figure in his day. He had had the conventional career of the young naval officer, Dartmouth, midshipman, courses, and had then passed into the submarine service.

Like most of his generation, Connor embraced convention, needed it. It was psychologically essential to him. His father

37

had been a painter. Whenever Connor said this, he said, 'Of all things, a painter.' His father was an iconoclast, compulsively non-conformist and a wild man in Paris in the days of Dada.

The divorce of Connor's parents had only accentuated Connor's need for convention, the security of the accepted. His taste, his outlook were shaped by the need not to stray away from the typical standards of his fellows. There was something almost feminine in this generation's compulsion to do nothing but what they all did – though, of course, Connor would never have admitted it. The youths he knew could scarcely bear doing their hair differently, wearing different-shaped shoes, listening to other jazz modes, and none of them balked at the accepted patterns of behaviour. Iconoclasm simply baffled them, made them uneasy.

The Navy seemed an ideal career to Connor. He found rich satisfaction in its set values, its treasured trivialities, in its high purpose, its certainty and regularity. He loved the life afloat, essentially unvarying in big ships and small. He loved the precision with which every fixture, every item of stores and equipment, every cog of, say, an aircraft carrier was tabulated and provided for by Fleet Orders, just like every contingency of wind and weather, every necessity of seamanship, every nicety of protocol, every facet of the secular tradition. He was happy in barracks or training school. The rigid code, the silent mess breakfasts behind barriers of newspapers, the pink gins, the calibrations of seniority and the reminiscences were all admirable to him.

The only thing Connor feared was the loss of these certainties. It wasn't a conscious fear. Nothing, he was sure, could shake the established order of this universe and the principles it laid down. But sometimes the thought of a breakdown flitted through his mind. Perhaps this went back to some childhood association to do with his parents' dissent. At all events, the idea was profoundly disturbing to him. Connor was like a man who has accepted a dogma and cannot endure a weakness in it, let alone a contradiction.

This was why he had been so afraid when, to all appearances, Jason, his commanding officer, had failed to blow

Uranus's tanks in time and surface after the explosions.

For a moment, Connor had completely lost his bearings. Jason had done the wrong thing by cancelling Bailey's order. Then, when he had – with appalling and blameworthy delay, so it seemed – ordered the tanks to be blown and the engines full ahead, far too late, it had only seemed to confirm the breakdown in command. Connor had only recovered when Jason had explained why.

Jason pulled out one of the long drawers of the chart table and extracted a chart. He used a pair of dividers and a parallel rule and marked off a point in pencil. Connor looked at it. The chart was one of the Kanin Peninsula area at the entrance to the White Sea. The point Jason had marked was on the west coast of the peninsula, opposite the small seaport of Chizha.

Connor raised his eyes. Jason was looking at him. It seemed to Connor that Jason knew what was going through his mind. Connor said, 'Are you going to tell them where we are?'

Jason looked down at the chart, then leant up from the table. 'I don't know yet. I don't think so.' A faint shadow of pain came over his face. 'If they know they're fairly close in, they'll want to use the escape chambers, take a chance on getting ashore. Some of them might be tempted to, at any rate. We don't know what the off-shore shipping is like here. Since the sonar has gone we shan't find out. If the Russians picked some of them up —' He did not need to finish the sentence.

Connor said, 'What are you going to do?'

'We have to wait until the time limit for the operation is over. That will be at two o'clock this afternoon.'

'Then the Ministry of Defence will realize we're in trouble.'

'Yes,' Jason said.

Connor looked back at him. He had full confidence.

When the explosions occurred, Petty Officer Grimble, who was on watch on the lower deck of the main engine room, was thrown off his feet and rammed against a machine handle. At the same time, a heavy steel case with two of the sodium pressure indicators lurched over on to his right leg, crushing it. By

39

a miracle, Grimble did not lose consciousness. He heaved the case away and freed himself.

The nearest explosion had seemed to come from close to, perhaps from the reactor compartment which was next door. There was an acrid smell and smoke. The lights had gone out and Grimble immediately felt and heard the surge of water into the engine room. There was also an unusual loud hissing and the shouting and groaning of injured and trapped men.

Grimble had one impulse. He gripped his disabled leg behind the knee and flipped over into a crouching position. He was in water already and was reaching out, trying to get his bearings in the dark. His shoulder touched the machine handle behind him and he knew where he was and made a lifting lunge for the watertight door just aft. He reached the door but found he was having to squeeze through it – and froze, thinking he had mistaken some piece of framework among the machinery for the doorway. But the next moment his touch confirmed it was the doorway opening and he squeezed through. His leg felt as if it were being torn off. In the dark he could hear the sea boiling in fast after him.

Grimble knew that if he did not do one thing he would be dead in about a minute. With his free hand, he groped for the watertight door, found it and swung it inwards towards himself to shut it. He was grimacing, his teeth bared, neck tendons splayed. He let go his injured leg. Pain burnt up through his body. He reached the handles of the clips to lock the door and wrenched at them.

Only a minute or two had passed since the explosions. Grimble shouldered the door and managed to pull one of the clips partly across. But to his horror, the door would not shut completely. It was the obstruction which he had squeezed past on the other side. The air and water were hissing in at the bottom of the door.

Grimble felt that the ship's tilt towards the stern had worsened. In those few terrible moments in the dark, he managed to keep his head. The water was above his knees. Electrical contacts on the bulkheads spat small flashes as the water reached them. He groped and found an emergency light

40

switch. One tiny blessed light sprang on over his head. It shone on the black water swirling round him.

Grimble made a supreme effort. He could see the faint gleam of the steel ladder which led up from the middle of the compartment to the small compartment on the deck above. He waded through the water, gripping the torn dungarees on his leg and dragging it behind him. The water was up to his chest as he reached the ladder.

He took the hand-rails on either side and hauled himself up on his forearms. He was straining to move as fast as he could, his head pressed back digging deep into his shoulders. He reached the top. The upper compartment was in darkness. Grimble fell to the deck on hands and good knee, gropingly searching for the watertight hatch shutting off the upper compartment from the one below. As he found it and pulled it over, there was a muffled creak from below, as if something had given and a louder surge of water and air. In the darkness, Grimble turned the wheel, screwing down the hatch and making it secure. A few seconds afterwards, the whole ship jarred heavily with loud grating sounds as it hit the bottom. Grimble fell over sideways and lost consciousness.

In the confusion of noise and the effort to save himself, Grimble had not heard the two watertight doors which led into the compartment where he now was from its fore and after ends being slammed shut and secured. In the next compartment, forward of him, were the six men with Petty Officer Punchard. They had heard the water swirling in below them and shut the watertight doors leading to their compartment before Jason had given the order.

In the other compartment, immediately aft of Grimble's, Mechanical Engineer Beale had also heard the water entering below. He was farther away from the explosions. He had switched on the emergency lighting and waited, even after the clang of the six, farther forward, shutting their door had reached him. Then abruptly he had felt himself in terrible danger, slammed the door of his small compartment, the stern-most in the ship, and locked himself in. A moment later he began shouting down the intercom, inaudible beyond.

CHAPTER FOUR

THE NAVAL OPERATIONS ROOM at the Ministry of Defence was bright with afternoon sun. The occupants could hear the cries of the first starlings flying in and out of the great plane-trees outside. This was not the room to be used in war; that was deep under the ground below, beyond the sound of any starlings. Nor was it a room where famous admirals had mapped out battles, raids and bombardments as they had in the old Admiralty room across the way. This was the room in the new unified services Ministry, anonymous and strictly untraditional.

The windows of the room looked out on to the Embankment and the river and, to one side, on to the antiquated Victorian pile of the War Office. Over the northern portal it had been thought fit to leave the two gigantic and sootily naked women in stone who had squatted above it when it had been the entrance to the Board of Trade.

The building had, indeed, its own symbolism. It had been built to house eight Ministries. When work had started and the ground plan been enlarged it had been seen that it would hold only four Ministries. With half the structure up, the Second World War had broken out. The building had been turned into a gigantic air-raid shelter. At the end of that war work on it had been resumed. But by the time the building had come to completion it could only hold two Ministries, the Air Ministry and the Board of Trade. It now held one-sixth of the staff of one Ministry, the Ministry of Defence. Cynics proclaimed its device to be *Parkinsonius in excelsis*.

The clock on the Operations Room wall said 4 pm. There were eight officers in the room. Three of them were busy at routine tasks and paid no direct attention to the rest. Vice-Admiral Lucan, the Vice-Chief of Naval Staff, stood in front of the big chart. He was a bulky man with a prognathous jaw who habitually stood leaning slightly forward with his arms held away from his body. It was a wrestler's stance, and Angus Lucan had been a great wrestler in his day. Otherwise he had the mildness and abnegation of a bishop. With him were Captain Rickard, Director of Naval Operations, Captain Field, Deputy-Director, Commander Spencer, of the operations staff, who was Duty Officer, and Lieutenant-Commander Haley-Brown, Duty Signals Officer.

The room was quiet. The windows were open, but beyond the starlings, the sound of traffic was muffled and distant. Ratings and girls of the WRNS moved about taking messages and papers from one desk to another or using a telephone. Occasionally a messenger came in with signals. There was nothing unusual about the activities in the room except that a red light was alight over the door, showing that a conference of senior officers was in progress.

Captain Rickard took a step nearer to the chart. He picked up a pointer, turned to the others. Rickard was a slight man with fair hair and, at forty-one, young to hold his position.

'*Uranus*'s orders were to regain the south Barents Sea at best speed, submerged of course, through these positions.' His pointer rose and traced a course north-west, then due north between the 42nd and 44th parallels of longitude. The course was the shortest which could be taken to clear the Russian coast and led roughly mid-way between the Kanin Peninsula on the east and the Kola Peninsula on the west. Rickard's pointer moved to a spot two-thirds of the way towards the Kola side.

'The traffic from Arkhangelsk and the other ports on the White Sea usually takes a course which divides about here, almost due east of the Cape Orlov light on the Kola side. Ships moving east from there along the north Russian coast, whether they touch at intermediate ports or go straight through to Varnek and up to the Kara Sea, invariably steam on a direct bearing east of the Cape Orlov light to the light at Cape Kanin Nos, here, at the tip of the Kanin Peninsula, and then follow strictly the sixty-ninth parallel.'

The pointer described a rapid course along the Russian

coast. 'Westbound traffic follows the Kola Peninsula and the Finnish coasts.' Captain Rickard brought the pointer back to its axis over the entrance to the White Sea, then lifted it to a point north of this, well in international waters. 'At Point Z, here, we have *Curlew*.' He glanced round at the Vice-Admiral. Lucan nodded. *Curlew* was one of Lucan's special babies – a new trawler class with ultrasensitive sonar equipment for searching the ocean depths for which Lucan had fought hard and long.

'*Curlew*'s orders are to make sonar contact with *Uranus* as *Uranus* withdraws from the operation and passes through Point Z submerged. As soon as she has confirmed *Uranus*'s passage, she is to signal us. To provide for bad weather or mishap, *Uranus* was told to remain in this area submerged for thirty minutes. That ought to give *Curlew* time to make her sonar contact.'

Vice-Admiral Lucan said, 'How is *Curlew* to differentiate between *Uranus* and a Soviet submarine that might be there?'

'There is to be standard recognition procedure. Once she has picked up the submarine, *Curlew* is to make an underwater recognition signal. *Uranus* will reply and will turn away on a course 120. *Curlew* will then complete the recognition procedure with another signal, on which *Uranus* will alter course to 270.'

Lucan nodded.

'*Curlew* has reported that she has been at Point Z for two hours but has heard nothing. She has made no sonar contact with *Uranus*. *Uranus* should have passed through the area an hour ago at the latest.'

Lucan's eyes were on the chart. Rickard could observe no change in expression on the massive face. He had seen Lucan with this same, almost benign, look at the worst imaginable moments.

'We are confident that there are no inshore mines?'

'Yes, sir.'

'Can we have DNI in?' Lucan said. Commander Spencer turned and gave an order to a petty officer. The petty officer went smartly out. While they waited, Lucan spoke quietly with Rickard, then leafed through a bundle of signals. Spencer watched his huge fingers turning the sheets over.

A captain entered the room and came up to the group. He was dark and hairy; there were tufts of hair in mid-cheek, tufts in his nose and ears, his eyebrows were craggy and his shaving area dark blue. He was Captain Harvey Ludovick, Director of Naval Intelligence.

They all waited until the Vice-Admiral had done with the signals. He looked up. 'DNI, *Uranus* is overdue. How good is your information that there are no inshore mines?'

Captain Ludovick allowed his glance to flicker rapidly over the faces of Commander Spencer and Lieutenant-Commander Haley-Brown. He seemed to be verifying the advisability of their hearing what he might say. 'We have a man who is in Kem at intervals. Kem is a good distance away, in the Karelo-Finnish Soviet Republic, but it is about the nearest one can get to Kanin; and he is an excellent informant. The data he has given us have been highly reliable.'

'Yes.'

'The Russians have laid sonar buoys at some points but, as far as we can find out, they do not go up there.'

The Vice-Admiral nodded.

Rickard said, 'The SRS2 would show any conventional underwater defences.' This was the Submarine Radarscope, a new piece of equipment which translated nets, booms and obstructions into blips on a scope as ordinary radar did above the surface. But it would not operate below a comparatively shallow depth.

'What about a collision?'

'Anything's possible, I suppose, sir. She'd have to hit something as she was coming up to use the periscope. The chances are small. There is not all that movement in the area.'

Captain Rickard turned to Haley-Brown. 'There's a procedure for a secondary signal, isn't there?'

'Yes, sir,' Haley-Brown said. 'If the rendezvous with *Curlew* fails, we notify *Uranus* that *Curlew* has heard nothing of her. When *Uranus* receives this signal she is to come to periscope depth, extend aerial and transmit a short series of QAs

45

and the code word Sextant in one cipher group. She will use ultra-long wave which would make it harder for the Russians to get a quick fix.'

Vice-Admiral Lucan said, 'You've sent your signal?'

'Yes, sir. It went at 1302, that's an hour ago. We're repeating it at fifteen-minute intervals. But there's been no acknowledgement.'

'There may be some reason why she wants to clear the area without replying – Soviet trawlers, something fortuitous. Or they may have something stalking her and she knows it. There might be . . .' Lucan left the sentence incomplete, as if he need not go on.

In the momentary silence there was a loud burst of sound from the starlings outside.

Commander Spencer sensed the uneasiness that had grown up among the group. They all stood looking at the chart. They could each of them find half a dozen reasons, Spencer knew, for *Uranus* not making her whereabouts known. Yet none of the reasons would carry intimate conviction. From long experience of the sea and ships they all sensed that something had gone wrong. Yet none of them could voice it. They would hardly admit it to themselves while there was hope.

Vice-Admiral Lucan said, 'Go on making your signal. Inform me immediately if there is a response.' He turned and went towards the door. Rickard went with him.

'I am going to tell the First Sea Lord,' Lucan said. 'Keep your staff here.'

Electrical Mechanic Farrel climbed down the ladder from the space at the top of *Uranus*'s fin to the bridge.

'No luck, sir,' he said to Jason. 'All we can get is Petty Officer Punchard's lot but nothing else.' He and Doggart, who was in the control room, had been trying to raise an answer from the two after compartments of the engine room through the intercom set at the top of the fin. Doggart had been following and testing the connection below. 'Looks as if the connection's broken somewhere where it runs through on the lower engine-room deck.'

46

'All right, Farrell,' Jason said.

'Yes, sir.' Farrell hesitated. His eye went to the signals on the chart table. He was obviously about to ask a question; but Doggart called up from below and there were steps on the ladder.

'Thank you, Farrell,' Jason said and turned away. As Connor appeared up the ladder, Farrel moved back to let him past, then went down himself.

Connor glanced at Jason. When the man was out of earshot, he said, 'What's the matter with Farrell? He looked a bit emotional.'

'He was going to ask where we are. Who can blame him, poor devil?'

Connor moved to the chart table. 'Trimmer is in pretty bad shape. They've made him as comfortable as they can and he's a tough egg and doesn't complain. His legs and right side are badly burned. We can't do much.'

'There's some morphine in the wardroom first-aid box.'

Connor nodded. 'We'll save it.'

'Take the key. How are the rest?'

'They'll do. Bloody good lot. Farrell's upset, as you see, and Monkhouse has had one or two vomits but he's doing his best. They're all right.' Jason and Connor had agreed that the men should be given the wardroom and control room as accommodation. Lieutenant Bailey was with them. Jason and Connor would share the space in the fin.

'Are they smoking?' Jason asked.

'You'd think so, wouldn't you? But not one of them has yet.'

The scrubber was working steadily. Jason was toying with a pair of dividers. He had again taken the chart out of the drawer and was contemplating it.

Connor said suddenly, 'Do you think we can get away with this?'

Jason looked up. He waited for Connor to go on.

'Surely there have been bodies blown out—and debris, oil. We're only five miles from the Russian coast. There are bound to be coastal craft about. Besides, if this shore installation is as

47

important as all that, there's probably a seaward lookout or a patrol or something.'

Jason said, 'There's a tremendous set just here, about seven knots. That has carried any debris well away to seaward. Bodies come up or they don't, you can't tell, especially with a set of that strength. They might not surface until they were miles away.'

'But the Russians must have aircraft patrols over here sometimes.'

'If they do it's probably high-altitude stuff. Intercepts for U2s and so forth. Miles up. Wouldn't see the sea.'

Connor said, 'Well, you'd think if they do it for intruder aircraft, they do it for subs too.'

'Maybe they do,' Jason said. 'We're hardly in a position to stop 'em.'

Connor glanced up. Jason's smile was grimly sardonic. He was relaxed, leaning with one elbow on the chart table. He might have been in Portland wardroom listening to a good but rather unlikely story.

Connor felt baffled. He had picked up a ball-point pen and was snapping the spring top in and out. Abruptly he said, 'Are you going to tell the ship's company?'

Jason turned his head away. He spread the dividers contemplatively on the chart. 'I don't know yet. I don't know. Christ! I wish I did.' He faced Connor. The smile had gone. There was a look of torment in his eyes. 'Wouldn't you want to try a swim? If you knew? Do you think they'll be put off indefinitely if I tell them there's a heavy current and they won't make it? Anyway, my strict orders are not to tell them.'

'But what then? We can't sit here and wait till we pass out.'

Jason said quietly, 'Can't we, Jack?'

'I —'

'Have you thought about what this means? What our presence here means? What are we going to save by saving ourselves? Nothing. We're only going to make it very much worse for people at home. In the situation we're in, the best thing that can happen is for us to pass out and for nobody to discover what happened to the ship.'

Connor met Jason's eyes. They were icy. Mentally, Connor recoiled. With all his love for the service, his admiration for Jason, it was too cold, too inhuman.

'Don't you see that?' Jason's voice cut at him.

'You can't do it.'

'I think it's my duty; and I think it's yours.'

Connor said, 'If we nurse the scrubber and keep it going we can probably last six or seven days. The Ministry knows we're lost now. They will do something. They have to.'

'In six days the carbon dioxide build-up is going to eliminate all our problems. Give it seven days at the outside. There's a little extra oxygen in the emergency breathing gear we can use.'

Jason moved across the tiny space of the bridge and back. In the forward bulkhead over the chart table were the two portholes fitted with glass thick enough to withstand great pressure. Beyond the glass there was darkness and the faint reflection of the lighted interior of the bridge and the two men.

Connor said, 'Can't we make a brief emergency signal? The Ministry must be keeping continuous radio watch. They know our position.'

'We've been told not to transmit.'

'Clyde —' It was the first time since the crash that Connor had used Jason's Christian name; it was a moment of appeal. But as soon as Connor had said it, he seemed to withdraw again. 'The orders don't say we're not to transmit; they're silent about it, they're – they're incomplete. They don't provide for these circumstances.'

'Perhaps not specifically. But everything in them makes it clear that we have to keep radio silence. Even if we *could* make a signal.'

'There's the EBSU —'

Jason snapped, 'I know there is, damn it! Don't you realize that if the Russians picked up a signal, they'd be out here with everything they've got and kill us? It's implicit in every line of the orders, every syllable, that we are not to disclose our presence to the Russians. It's simple enough to understand. Isn't it?'

'Yes. But even so —' Connor gritted his teeth. He wanted to protest, to say that the men could not be left to die without a chance; but he could not get it out. He could not speak. The void was opening before him again. The thought that the all-providing system had broken down, had failed to provide clear orders for this emergency, was shattering to him. He turned to the ladder. 'I – I'll go and see Trimmer,' he said and went down.

Jason did not move. He stood leaning over the chart. His shoulders were hunched, his neck sunk into them as if he were bracing himself. He ached for a cigarette. He felt himself torn as he had not been for long since in the struggle within himself. He knew he was right. But right and logic were terribly inadequate. He longed to share Connor's feelings, to find himself at one with Connor and the rest, even if he had, notwithstanding, to stick to the orders. It was strange that he should want to justify not his own attitude but to justify Connor's, yet that was how it was. He knew he could, if it came to it, remain silent and let the survivors now in the submarine be overcome by carbon dioxide poisoning. He was confident that he could enforce it on Connor too. But he was mortally afraid of it. Now he knew that what he was ultimately afraid of was finding that he was already dead inside. That was what he couldn't face; that was the discovery he was trying to stave off.

He took out a cigarette, then smashed it with a savage stab and threw it aside. Was it his duty to save the men or to sacrifice them coldly in the higher interests of the country? The muscle at the corner of his eye was twitching. He did not know the answer.

In the engine room, the five men with Petty Officer Punchard squatted or lay in different postures or eased their limbs. The light in the compartment was dim. Petty Officer Punchard had ordered only one emergency light alight at a time to save the battery.

Acre, the injured man, had most room; he was stretched out

50

full length between two banks of machinery. Tippett was squatting near his head. He had laid out a game with matches on the deck plating and was trying to keep Acre's attention on it.

'This one here? You can't do that, George. You're going to give the whole side away. Look, I mean . . . see?'

Acre rolled his head away as if he were too weary to pay any further attention; but the next moment he had turned back. He looked at Tippett with feeble gratitude. In a whisper he said, 'Sorry, Bert. You're right.'

Leading ME Vickers was chinning himself on a steel support.

'Take it easy, Vick,' Punchard said. 'You'll make us all of a sweat.'

'He thinks he's in the gym at 'ome,' Davis said. 'Didn't you know, Punch? He's got a whole wing of Branksome Towers, his country seat, for a gymnasium, ain't you, Vick? Billiard tables an' all. One of the show places of the 'Ome Counties, ain't it, Vick?'

Vickers was grinning. He let go and stood looking down at the other two. 'Maybe you're not far out there, neither. Y'know what I'm going to do when I sign out of this navy racket? I'm going in with my brother-in-law. Lovely little pub down at Congesbury, in Somerset. They call it Combesbury, the locals. He's been waiting on it seven years. A free house. It's got one of them skittle alleys out the back. The locals play with bloody great cartwheels they call cheeses. You get playing a couple of hours of that, boy, and you keep up a lovely thirst.'

'I could punish a pint of bitter right now without any skittles,' Davis said.

Punchard grinned. His adam's apple rose and descended.

'Think of bloody great pickled onions and a hunk of cheese.'

'And a crusty bit of cottage loaf,' Vickers said.

'Bottles of pickled onions, a sort of browny gold.'

'And a plate of tongue with 'em.'

'Crumbly, like, and hot mustard.'

There was a sort of musing murmur of recollection.

51

'Where's that geiger counter, Punchard?' Leading ERA Maxwell said in a loud voice. He was in the corner of the compartment. 'My skin's pricklin'. I told you we was all going to get fried by that bleedin' reactor. I can feel it.'

'That'll do from you, my lad,' Punchard said. 'There's no more radioactivity than there's ever been. I'm keeping a check and if there's any danger I'll let you know.' His fingers touched the geiger counter by his side. Vickers noticed that he didn't consult it. Punchard had taken it over at the beginning and wasn't letting it out of his sight.

'Yes,' Maxwell snarled. 'Then we can take a bath and go for three weeks' leave to Ilfracombe, I suppose.'

Nobody answered. The scrubber was working rhythmically.

'Talking about Ilfracombe,' Punchard said. 'Did I tell you about that waitress I got in tow with there?' He started a story but it didn't carry conviction or hold their attention and did nothing to dissipate the atmosphere of uneasiness. Vickers noticed that Acre had painfully twisted round and was watching Maxwell.

All at once, without a word, Davis, who was taking his turn in the confined space by the condenser, began stroking an imaginary dog. He ran his hands over the back of the head and down the backbone, pulled out the tail, scratched behind the ears, patted, lifted a paw, chuckled. '. . . good boy, good boy . . . what's the matter, eh? Blackie? Blackie?'

Quietly the others watched him. Nobody spoke. The imaginary dog had been a game on board. Long ago, Ransome, one of the cooks, had invented Blackie and the ship's company had quickly caught on, sensing the usefulness of a little fantasy, adopting it as a welcome note of relief in the life on board. Ransome had tacitly been recognized as the 'owner' but the dog had simultaneously 'belonged' to the ship in general. Everybody had used the joke and a complex lore and convention about Blackie had grown up.

Ransome had been one of the men lost in the disaster. Nobody had mentioned Blackie but now there seemed something uncomfortable and strange – something that had never hitherto attached to Blackie – about Davis's mimicking evocation of the dog. It was as if Davis had conjured up a ghost.

Davis was now pretending that Blackie was playfully snarling and growling. He pushed it away, he pulled it towards him, he rolled it over, he laughed. Then he made as if the dog had a stick between its jaws. He gripped the imaginary stick with both hands, worked it free, threw it across the compartment. The others squatted in awkward silence. Even Punchard looked uneasily at a loss.

'That's the boy, Blackie. Give it now. Come on . . .' Davis was snatching at the stick, as if the dog kept coming within reach then retreating. Then he caught the stick, held it up, the dog jumping after it.

The tension in the compartment had suddenly risen. Davis was laughing. He was so absorbed in the mimed game with the dog that he did not notice its effect. He yelped, as if the dog had nicked him, and the next minute was reaching out, trying to snatch the dog's legs.

'Hey, you little bastard, I'll have you for that. Where's that strap? Come here . . .'

'Oh, for Christ's sake, Davis! Stow it, can't you?' It was Tippett. His jaw was jutting and he was as white as paper. None of them had ever seen Tippett like that. He was usually one of the most even-tempered and best-humoured men in the crew. Davis turned pale. He dropped his hands, looked away. It was over in an instant.

Suddenly the scrubber faded out completely. There was dead silence. Everybody's eyes went to the vent. They were motionless.

Slowly Punchard rose to his feet, his eyes still on the vent. He went to it and reached up, holding the back of his hand a few inches from the vent to feel the flow of air. A startled look came into his eyes. Without warning the scrubber started again. The stone-like figures of the men moved, seemed, for an instant, to crumble with relief. Then they recovered.

'Where's that geiger counter, Punchard?'

'Pipe down, Maxwell,' Punchard said gently.

The scrubber had been momentarily cut out by Chief Petty

53

Officer Doggart who was working on the Emergency Buoy Signal Unit. This was the EBSU which Connor had referred to in the exchange with Jason. It consisted of a buoy equipped with a small radio transmitter which could be released from the submarine's hull in an emergency. It was intended to rise to the surface and transmit a fixed SOS to guide rescue ships; and since this safety device could, if it were misused, lead to the submarine's detection, a combination of security locks confined its use and prevented it being tampered with. The commanding officer kept the key and the EBSU was not controlled from the main control room switchboard, though it could be connected to it, but from the bridge.

Two hours before, Jason had sent for Chief Petty Officer Doggart. For an instant, as Doggart had reached the bridge, Jason's face had looked ravaged. But the look had passed quickly. Doggart was at first startled, then put it down to a transitory effect of the light.

'How are things, Chief?'

'Can't complain, sir.'

'How long is the emergency lighting good for?'

'Five or six days yet, sir. We're keeping it down.'

'We may go to long cruise routine.' It was standard practice on long submerged cruises in the nuclear submarines to use the lighting to mark the days and nights – switching on for the day and cutting to a glimmer at night. Jason and other commanders had found this helped the men bear the deadly monotony and gave a semblance of rhythm to their existence. Once *Uranus* had cruised submerged for fifty days and after the first month it had seemed like a thousand years. Time lost its meaning. Jason had found himself asking what day of the week it was, even with the lights going on and off. Now, above all, he wanted time to be measureless and this was why he had not already ordered the change to the cruise drill. But if it was going to extend the life of the batteries they must go over.

Jason turned away. He looked out at the black water beyond the porthole. Two hundred and seventy feet of it above them.

Doggart stood waiting expectantly. Jason faced round. 'Chief Petty Officer Doggart, do you think you could get the

EBSU to transmit a signal, not simply the automatic SOS?'

Doggart's eyes searched Jason's face; then he looked away. He drew his lips in reflectively; there were plainly many things going through his mind and he was puzzled. 'Might be able, sir. I can't tell.'

'In principle, can it be done?'

'In principle, I dare say. Trouble is, I've got no spares, no stores items, or practically none.'

'Will you see if it's possible, Chief?'

'Yes, sir.' Doggart was looking at him intently again, the perplexity more evident. Jason could see he was asking himself why the EBSU was not up and transmitting its SOS already.

Jason said, 'You see what I'm after? Since we can't surface I want to use the EBSU as our transmitter. For the moment I only want to send a short signal and I want to keep the EBSU just below the surface. If we can keep the antenna from breaking water, all but the extreme tip, so much the better.'

'Of course it's not meant for that, sir. The EBSU is —'

'I know, Chief. We have to do the best we can. I have unlocked the panel above, the safety catch and the slip ring here. Will you get to work straight away?'

For a moment, Doggart hung there obviously wanting to ask a lot of questions. But he said, 'Aye, aye, sir,' saluted and turned away. He reached for the ladder to go down.

'Oh, Chief,' Jason said, 'perhaps it won't work, so I'd say nothing to the others. You'll need a mate, but that's all. We don't want to raise false hopes.'

'No, sir,' Doggart said. 'I understand, sir.'

'Report what the prospects are as soon as you can.'

'Yes, sir.' Doggart went down.

Leading Radio Operator Kirby was off watch. Doggart took him as his mate. Part of the EBSU mechanism was accommodated in a cupboard-like recess off the control room, still accessible, and it extended up through the fin to the after part of the space above the bridge. When Doggart and Kirby had been working on it for an hour, Doggart came down from above and said to Jason that they thought the job could be done. But he was seriously troubled by Jason's insistence that the modified EBSU would have to transmit without being fully on the surface. He wanted to find out why this was necessary and Jason had to deflect his curiosity without making him suspicious.

Half an hour later, Doggart reappeared and said it would be necessary to dismantle an item of gear used in transmitting the fixed SOS. 'I wouldn't like to say we can get it to work if we have to put it back, sir. I'm short of wiring.'

'Dismantle it,' Jason said without hesitation.

'Aye, aye, sir.'

When Doggart had gone, Jason took out the cipher books and began to encipher a message to the Ministry of Defence. Doggart had moved temporarily to the space in the fin immediately below the bridge and Kirby was working in the control-room recess. Somebody below lit a cigarette and the pleasant tang floated up to Jason. He flicked over the cipher-book pages, looking up the groups. It didn't take long. He leant against the bulkhead. His reflection stared at him from the porthole.

He heard Doggart's voice far away. He seemed to be swimming up from vast and unfathomable depths. The light became dirty grey with a bloody tinge. His limbs moved heavily. He felt a weight on his shoulders and lifted his head, reaching towards the air and light with the confused image of a turtle in his mind. He could not lift his eyelids. Suddenly he was hearing Doggart's voice more clearly.

'Captain, sir.'

Jason sat up. He opened his eyes and looked at the clock. He had been asleep for one hour and fifteen minutes. 'Please,' he said. His mouth was cindery. Doggart was there.

'EBSU's fixed up, sir. As best we can, at any rate. With a bit of luck we might get a signal away. Can't guarantee it, sir.' Doggart was dirty and obviously tired.

'Thank you, Chief. Send Kirby up. I have the signal ready.'

CHAPTER FIVE

THE POLICEMAN ON duty at the door of 10 Downing Street saluted the tall uniformed figure, taller than himself, which bent forward, jack-knifed itself out of the official car and straightened to a grotesque height. The First Sea Lord returned the salute. The saluting hand seemed to float, to hover over the helmet of the tall policeman. The First Sea Lord had owed some of his success to his stature. He was the tallest man in British naval history.

As he crossed the pavement, the venerable boom of Big Ben striking the hour came on the wind. The First Sea Lord had driven from the House where he had expected to find the Prime Minister. But the Prime Minister had left and the First Sea Lord had come to Number 10. There had been rain and the roads were glistening.

The First Sea Lord passed into the building. The door-keeper in the blue Office of Works uniform said, 'Good evening, sir.'

'Good evening, Smithers,' the First Sea Lord said.

He crossed the black-and-white-tiled entrance hall, passing the second policeman there, and took the long corridor opposite, leading to the Prime Minister's room. He strode down the red carpet with long steps. Unseeingly his eye took in the busts – Pitt, Melbourne, Disraeli – the photographs of past Cabinets and Imperial Conferences. At the end of the corridor was another hallway which formed the ante-room where Ministers and visitors waited to see the Prime Minister.

The First Sea Lord turned towards the left-hand corner which was partly screened off and contained table, chairs and fireplace. It was customary to wait here.

Almost immediately, Adrian Henning, the Principal Private Secretary, came out and greeted the Admiral with a quiet 'Good evening'. He was a wrinkled-browed youngish man with a long lean face, the head of the Prime Minister's personal staff of seven, and had been expecting the Admiral after the telephone call from the House. His glance indicated a chair. 'I'll see if the coast is clear,' he said.

The First Sea Lord nodded but remained standing. He was not a man to take chairs casually. He looked round the ante-room. The white marble head of Wellington regarded him from a niche by the fireplace. Count Bothmar looked at him from a print. The First Sea Lord had never known who Count Bothmar was and didn't greatly care. He had always thought the ante-room a damned curious place and that it must fill a stranger with a sense of being neither here nor there.

In a moment, the door on his left opened and Henning said, 'Will you come in, First Sea Lord. He will be back at once.' As the First Sea Lord moved through the doorway into the large rectangular room dominated by the great table, the phone rang in Henning's adjoining office. Henning let the First Sea Lord get well into the room, said 'Excuse me,' and, withdrawing into his office, shut the door.

The famous room which, by tradition, was not only the Prime Minister's office but also the Cabinet Room, was familiar enough to the First Sea Lord. His eye roamed over the long green-baize-covered table, surrounded by chairs, the muddy portrait of Walpole over the fireplace beyond, the Corinthian columns, the folded newspapers on the side table, the two tall curtained windows at the far end. The brass chandeliers were alight. The mahogany and black leather chairs gleamed. They had restored the original light eighteenth-century panelling in the redecoration and it looked very elegant.

The Prime Minister's chair, the only armchair at the table, was pushed back. The stub of a single cigarette lay in the glass ashtray. A few things only distinguished the Prime Minister's place from the rest – the single green-handled scrambler tele-phone, the panel of seven buzzers for his staff, a silver tray of pencils, the small brown desk-lamp and a propped-up postcard with engagements. No in-trays, no piles of papers, no note-books or dispatch cases.

The door opened and the Prime Minister came in. 'Admiral,' he made a small gesture with his hand. 'You said it was urgent?'

The First Sea Lord thought he looked – how would you put it? – almost fatherly, he had heard people say; not paternal, certainly nothing of the heavy touch or the patronism that implied, but deeply experienced, with an inner calm and toughness gained in hard decisions and crushing responsibilities. There had been disappointments and humiliations enough in the Prime Minister's political life; but his personal demeanour had seemed to gain from them. There was nothing particularly formal about him, the First Sea Lord thought again; yet his dignity in the political warfare through which he had led his party and the country seemed more than a personal attribute, more than political wisdom. It had symbolized something finer and conveyed that relaxed, friendly, unhurried – damn it, fatherly sureness that made his political contemporaries look small and paltry. (Lesser men would, in any event, have long since been obliterated.) It was a quality which, with his sincerity, his honesty, his Olympian generosity, had stopped Opposition offensives against him dead in their tracks. Trial had only lifted him, emphasized his elevation of thought, his ignorance of meanness and his ruggedness.

The Prime Minister took his place at the long table and gestured to the First Sea Lord to take the next chair. This was the customary position for all visitors. There was no 'sitting out' area in the room.

The First Sea Lord sat down. The Prime Minister took a cigarette from a small gold case holding about four.

'I'm sorry not to bring you good news, Prime Minister,' the Admiral said. '*Uranus,* the nuclear submarine we sent to scan the shore installations the Russians have set up east of Murmansk, is overdue. She was to have carried out two signalling procedures to notify us that she had completed the mission but hasn't done so. Altogether she is now several hours overdue.'

The Prime Minister had lit his cigarette which he smoked without inhaling. 'You've no news at all? No indication of what's become of the ship?'

'Nothing.'

'What is your conjecture?'

'It's impossible to tell. The ship was under orders to keep radio silence and she was proceeding submerged the whole way, since the operation meant going into Russian territorial waters.'

The Prime Minister's expression underwent no change. The First Sea Lord felt a flicker of relief. Authority for the operation had been sought in the normal way, of course. The risks had been set forth, the advantages, indeed the necessity, in the eyes of the Defence Staff, of knowing more about the Chizha installations had been explained. It had all gone through ultimately to the Prime Minister who alone could give the sanction.

Yet there had been the faint lurking chance that the implications had not registered at that final top political level. In the immense pressure of public business, the Prime Minister had perhaps – perhaps – given the nod somewhat automatically, basing himself, as he had a right to, on the expert opinions of the Admirals, Field Marshals and Air Marshals of the Defence Staff. It had happened before. It was indeed not unusual political currency, just as Ministers necessarily found themselves 'covering' decisions which had been taken by the permanent civil servants.

The sheer complexity of government affairs, the appalling paperwork, the relentless shouldering of time and public engagements made it impossible to sit back reflectively for long on a particular issue. And even with the Prime Minister's great political flair it was possible to miss a relevancy, a latent contingency. So that seeing the Prime Minister sitting there unmoved by full cognisance, the First Sea Lord felt an anxiety fall from his mind.

'Yes. I see,' the Prime Minister said thoughtfully.

The door to the adjoining office at the end of the room opened and Henning came in. He went past the First Sea Lord and spoke to the Prime Minister. 'The Naval Operations Room is on the telephone for the First Sea Lord. I said he was with you but they are asking permission to speak urgently.'

'Of course,' the Prime Minister said.

The First Sea Lord unfolded himself and rose. Henning unhooked the telephone from the table and handed it to him. 'Yes? This is the First Sea Lord.' He listened. Almost at once, his towering form became very still. The corners of his mouth tightened. The voice at the other end, a harsh metallic voice, could be heard from the earpiece. 'Yes. Very well ...' the First Sea Lord said. 'Do so. Thank you.' His tone was crisply decided. But in curious contrast, he reached out with almost painful slowness to put the phone back. There was the click of the Operations Room caller ringing off before it reached the cradle. He looked at the Prime Minister.

'There has been a signal from *Uranus*,' he said. 'She is extensively damaged and disabled, with twenty-nine known survivors, including the commanding officer, inside the operating zone.'

The Prime Minister extended an arm and tapped the ash of his cigarette into an ashtray. Then on second thoughts, he stubbed the half-smoked cigarette out. He said quietly, 'Good God.' It was as if he were speaking to himself. He looked up at the First Sea Lord. 'That means inside Soviet territorial waters?' Did the question, perhaps, carry a fragmentary hope that he was wrong?

'Yes,' the First Sea Lord said.

There was a moment's silence. The First Sea Lord said, 'The signal was incomplete. She started to give the exact position but broke off. It seemed to be some improvised emergency procedure. It is possible to fix the approximate position she's in. The operating area is just south-west of Chizha and we directed her course. She's in about forty-five fathoms.'

Suddenly the lines on the Prime Minister's face seemed deeper. He got to his feet. 'Is it genuine? Can it be a trap?'

The First Sea Lord saw that he was utterly shaken. The Prime Minister turned to face him and once again there was the note of appeal in his voice. 'Are you sure the signal was from *Uranus*? Can we be sure?'

'I think there's no doubt, Prime Minister,' the First Sea Lord said.

The Prime Minister pushed back his chair and moved to the end of the long table. He said something to himself in a low voice without turning his back.

There was sympathy and pain in the First Sea Lord's eyes. His glance went round the gracious room where so many hard decisions had been taken. There were times when it seemed to a seafaring man too elegantly divorced from the hideous alternatives that now confronted them all in the world.

The Prime Minister faced round. 'How long can they hold out?'

'We don't know. They haven't given any indication. If the air system is working, or part of it, they might last for days. If by some chance it is intact, they could last for weeks.'

'Weeks!' The Prime Minister's voice was ghostly. He moved forward to the window, parted the curtain with his hand and stared out. He turned back to the First Sea Lord.

'What can be done?'

'If the government decides to disregard the territorial limit, Prime Minister, the Navy will go in with good heart. I'm bound to say that a rescue operation of that sort would attract immediate attention and unless the Russians agreed to co-operate or were at least benevolently inclined, I don't see what could be done. To try something without telling the Russians would be fraught with danger – great danger.'

In other words, it was a political decision. It was out of his province, the First Sea Lord was saying. He could put it no plainer.

'Of course,' the Prime Minister said, as if that were understood. After a moment's thought, he said, 'Is the submarine capable of receiving radio signals?'

'If they have a transmitter working, it's on the cards they can.'

'And it is possible for them to escape at that depth?'

'Yes, they can get up with escape gear.'

The Prime Minister squared himself. The deeply set eyes in which many had tried to read thoughts and intentions were fixed on the First Sea Lord's. 'Send a signal to the submarine,

First Sea Lord. She is to keep radio silence until further notice.'

Able Seaman Wingrove was stripped to a pair of briefs. He sat on one of the mess-room tables, his massive torso and legs glistening like a wrestler's. His fat good-natured face was equally sweaty. His thighs spread gigantically under his weight. A momentary lull had settled on the compartment after a noisy dispute about when they would use the escape hatch.

Bosco had deserted Petty Officer Fitch and changed his allegiance to Haynes. He now called Haynes 'Dave'. And a bloody fine pair too, Petty Officer Robertson thought. Haynes had discovered a cut-throat razor in one of the mess cupboards and was stropping it on the edge of his palm. Fitch and Cubit sprawled at the other end of the table.

'Bosco's right. There must be signals coming in,' Green said. He was squatting on the deck.

'Evans says the radio's been working nineteen to the dozen ever since we got down here,' Bosco said. 'What's the idea of keeping it quiet from us?'

'How do you know what Evans says?' Robertson couldn't help saying. Evans was supposed to be one of the survivors in the control room, according to the rumours.

'Ah, shut up for Christ's sake, Robbie.'

It was incredible to Robertson how rumours kept going round, even with the ship disabled and some of the compartments flooded. Bosco and Cubit were the worst. They were always coming up with some new buzz. They both swore they had reports from other sections of the ship over the intercom. Robertson didn't believe them. The buzzes only made the atmosphere worse. Cubit said there were no officers left alive in the ship except the Captain and Connor and that it was bluff about Bailey being in the control room. Robertson couldn't see this at all. Then Bosco had started swearing about the signals that he said were coming in from the Ministry of Defence.

'Honest, when we going to get orders to go, Dave?' Green

said, trying to get back to escape.

'Ask Robbie; he knows what's a good buzz and when you're just being a tuckin' great liar.' It was a small challenge. Haynes, a skilful trouble-maker, had long since sensed Robertson's antagonism. Robertson let it go. He wasn't playing Haynes's game.

Savage put his head and shoulders through from the torpedo compartment. 'It's still dripping, Robbie.'

'Suppose you stop drippin', you stupid bastard?' Bosco said.

'That's enough, Bosco.' Robertson got to his feet.

'What's it to you, Robbie?' Haynes said, looking up. Their eyes met. Haynes twisted the razor so that the open blade glinted.

'Only that I'm Petty Officer here,' Robertson said, calmly. 'See?'

They were still staring at each other. Haynes smiled broadly and defiantly up into Robertson's face and suddenly all the others laughed out loud. It was a laugh against Robertson and Robertson knew it.

'Robbie,' Savage jerked at his arm. Robertson turned away. He was under control. But the situation was getting no better.

In the torpedo compartment, Savage was pointing to a small pool of water on the deck plating. A drop fell from the piping above.

'Condensation,' Robertson said.

'But Robbie, that's one of those outlets they were working on in the dockyard. It's the one with the faulty sea-valve and I swear that's —'

'Take it easy, boy.' Robertson reached up, put his palm on the damp piping, shook his head. 'It's condensation, Savage. Here, have a smoke.'

Suddenly the Tannoy speaker became live with an electric hum and sounds of somebody handling the mike at the other end. They turned towards the speaker grille. Robertson could see Fitch and Cubit suddenly sitting up in the mess. They stopped talking.

The voice came over. 'Ship's company, this is the Captain

speaking. Captain speaking to ship's company. You're all getting through this pretty well. I wanted to tell you we've got a signal away. Our position's known and if anything can be done to help us, it will be. The gauges, as you see, show we are in two hundred and seventy feet of water. The scrubber is working well and it looks like going on.'

There was a break; then the voice resumed. 'You are all asking yourselves where we are. You were not, I may say, supposed to know. But we've run into trouble and I am going to take the responsibility of telling you. I want you to understand that there is no question of *your* responsibility in this. If certain things happen and you find yourselves being interrogated, you may answer that you are not in any way to be held responsible. You were carrying out the orders of your officers and superiors.

'I am also telling you to put you on your guard against giving away details about the ship and her equipment and your work in her if you are picked up by the Russians. We are in Soviet territorial waters. You can all see what this means. It increases our difficulties and dangers. We may be attacked. We can't signal freely. Above all, we can't use the escape chambers yet. If we did, the Russians might pick us up. You notice I say *might*. The position we are in happens to be a bad one for individual or collective escape without help from rescue craft on the surface because there's a very strong current. Anybody who reached the surface would be swept out to sea. It would take a very strong swimmer indeed several hours to reach the coast – if he could make it. That is one reason why we can't use the escape chambers.

'There's another reason. If the Russians pick us up and locate the ship, it is going to bring on a very grave crisis between our country and Russia. We can't foresee the consequences. We are not on an aggressive mission. But we could easily seem to be and once the Russians decided we had been sent to attack them, it would be hard to convince them otherwise.

'Is that clear? We were *not* going to attack the Russians. But they probably wouldn't believe us. It's no good guessing

65

what they would do. But you see that it all goes a great deal beyond us, beyond what finally happens to us. On us may depend what subsequently happens not only to our own families at home but to many thousands of others – maybe millions. For these reasons, no man will use the escape chambers until I give the order. Nothing is to be dumped out of the waste disposal. Any suspected oil leak is to be reported at once. Whatever can be done for us is going to be done. You needn't doubt that. Until then we have to stick it out. You've all got guts and I know you will. That's all.'

The loudspeaker clicked off. There was silence. Savage was staring at Robertson with his mouth open. Robertson's eyes were fixed unseeingly on the NOT LOADED plate hanging from the torpedo tube. Wingrove was looking in at them from the door.

Bosco's voice from the mess said, 'Russian waters. Well, for Christ's sake.' There was some swearing and Robertson and Savage stepped through into the mess. They all stood looking at each other, an almost motionless tableau in the dim glow of the emergency light, their eyes trying to read each other's thoughts, heads turning slowly from one to the other of the group.

'It doesn't change anything,' Robertson said. 'All we got to do is to take it easy and stay put.'

'What?' Fitch's face was pale with anger. 'All we're supposed to do is to sit and wait for the bloody Russians to knock us off?'

'Who said they're going to knock us off?' Robertson said loudly and strongly. 'Have a bit of sense, man, you ought to be —'

'He said so!'

'The Old Man just said it.'

'He wouldn't've told us unless we're going to get it.'

The tension had snapped and they were all speaking at once.

'What right's he got to stop us getting out?'

'You heard what he said.'

'Does he know what current there is out there . . .?'

'. . . supposed to be in the Atlantic . . .'

'If we don't do what he said . . .'

'Just an excuse . . .'

'Shut up! Shut up, all of you.' Suddenly they were all looking at Haynes – the intense, intelligent, straining face, the fair hair, the hard mouth with the corners turning down and the curious mingling of cocksureness and cunning in his expression.

Haynes looked round at them in silence. He did so deliberately for effect. It was as if he had brought them to order and now he was going to *tell* them. As disgustedly as he could, Robertson said 'Christ!'

'What are we *doing* in Russian waters?' Haynes said. 'Why doesn't he tell us that? He says it's not our responsibility. But we've got to take the consequences – and we still don't know what we're doing.'

'Sitting on the bottom,' Robertson said. 'What else does it look like?'

'I suppose that's what we came here for, Petty Officer? Can the Petty Officer tell us?' It was the perfect sea-lawyer's manner. Haynes's face was thrust forward. Robertson was sickened but there was a growl of assent from Fitch, Bosco and Cubit.

'Because if he can't, I can,' Haynes went on. 'If we're to believe our commanding officer and we've not come here to attack the Russians, then we're here for one thing – spying.'

A moment's silence. 'Isn't it obvious?' Haynes said. 'Why else do you send a submarine into Russian territorial waters? Why does our commanding officer tell us a pack of lies about trials in the Atlantic? Because he's hoodwinking us. And he's been hoodwinking us under orders, which makes it worse. I knew there was something funny about this trip all along. I told you so. What right have they got to make spies out of us —?'

'Haynes,' Robertson said, 'I'm warning you not to go on with this line of talk. If you —'

'Aw shut up, Robbie,' Cubit said.

'Stow it!' Fitch, Bosco and Green shouted at him together, siding with Haynes.

'I'm senior PO, if you want to make anything of it,' Fitch

said, jerking his chin up. 'Go on, Haynes.' It was Fitch's own surrender to Haynes in the guise of patronage. Haynes was now their ringleader.

Wingrove, who was standing next to Robertson, ostentatiously put his arm round Robertson's shoulder and was going to move him away. But Robertson shook his head. They stayed where they were.

Haynes was continuing. 'I didn't sign any agreement to be a spy. Did you, Bosco? You, Cubit?'

Cubit said, 'Spy? Who knows if those Polaris tubes are really empty?'

Robertson blew his breath out, as if he smelled a bad smell, and there was a deprecatory murmur from Green and Savage.

'What do you mean?' Green said. 'There hasn't been any firing drill since we sailed. That missile compartment hasn't been manned.'

'We were bluffed on this trip, weren't we? They told us lies about exercising in the Atlantic. Why shouldn't they tell lies about the missile compartment being empty?'

'Who's from missiles here?' Bosco said, looking round. 'Who's got action stations on missiles?' Nobody responded.

'You mean we might have been out to attack the Russians?' Fitch said.

'Why not?' Cubit looked tougher and more confident, Robertson thought. The impression of resentment he often gave was gone. The peculiar bunched muscles at the angles of his jaw were working excitedly.

Haynes, who had been silent for a moment, said, 'You're talking bull, Cubit. For one thing, if we're in Russian waters already and we were going to attack, the missile boys would've been at stations. But if we were really going to attack, we'd be crazy to go near Russian waters. We'd stay away. That's the whole idea.'

'No it ain't, that's *your* idea. Did you make the rules? Anyhow, how do you know the missile boys weren't closed up at stations?'

Haynes gave him a close look. 'We weren't; and we would've been too.'

Cubit made a gesture of scornful dismissal.

'All right, all right, make what you want of it. But there's one thing that's obvious to me – it's spying,' Haynes said. 'What right has the Ministry of Defence to get us into this?'

'No bloody right.'

'And now we're supposed to play dominoes or read a good book till we pass out or the Russians blow us to Jesus.'

'What d'you want, Haynes, danger money?' Wingrove said and laughed. Green and Savage grinned, but caught Haynes's eye and looked away. Haynes flicked Wingrove a glance. He gave a sort of sour disdainful grin.

'Why don't you call up the Old Man and ask him?' Fitch said. Perhaps he didn't think Haynes would do it, Robertson thought.

Haynes looked round the group. 'All right.' He went over to the Tannoy, threw the switch so that the reply would come through on the loudspeaker and said, 'Calling the bridge.'

'Captain,' Jason's voice said.

'Leading Seaman Haynes speaking.' The lack of the 'sir' was like a shout. 'We want to know why we're in Russian waters.'

'I'm sure you do, Haynes.' Jason's voice was gentle and understanding. 'It's natural enough that you should, but it's something I can't tell you. You may take my word for it that it wasn't for any aggressive purpose.'

'Spying isn't aggressive?'

Jason let it pass; he didn't answer.

'We ought to have been told we were coming into Russian waters,' Haynes said.

'Leading Seaman Haynes, I think you're making some mistaken assumptions. Secret orders are a commonplace. We've all sailed this ship a dozen times without anybody but myself knowing our course, our destination, how long we'd be away and what we were going to do. You know that perfectly well, since you've been in the ship. It happens daily elsewhere. The officers who made out our orders this time had no more reason to explain further than they have on those other occasions.'

'But this is spying and we didn't join the service to spy.'

'Who are "we"?'

'Some of us here. Any of us here, for that matter.'

'You're expected to carry out orders, Haynes. You as well as the rest of us. I don't see any point in pursuing this line of talk. Put the senior PO on.'

Haynes paused, tightlipped, then handed over to Fitch.

'PO Fitch, sir.'

'Petty Officer Fitch, what's happening in your section?'

'Everything in order, sir.'

'It doesn't sound like it. See that this intercom is not used except for its proper purpose. You're in charge of it and you're to communicate over it and nobody else. Is that clear?'

'Yes, sir.' Jason rang off.

Haynes sat on the table, lit a cigarette. 'It just confirms we've been tricked into this, that's all.' Cubit and Bosco nodded.

'From what you say, you'd think the Russians never did any spying,' Robertson said.

'Would you? Did I say they didn't?'

Cubit flared up. 'If they do they leave it to professionals. Haynes is right, we didn't agree to this sort of dirty work, sneak-thieving in here.'

'I suppose you expect the Admiral to ask your permission first,' Robertson said. 'Is it all right by you, Leading ME Cubit, if we do so and so?'

'Ah, go and —' Green and Savage joined in the chorus.

Bosco said something in Haynes's ear and Haynes nodded.

'What we going to do, Dave?' Savage said.

Haynes spat out a crumb of tobacco. His lips turned down into a contemptuous grin.

CHAPTER SIX

THE SECOND CAR arrived at 10 Downing Street at 9.10 pm, twelve minutes after the first. The man who got out was not obviously hurried but did not waste time. He took the single step across the pavement with his head down. The policeman on duty caught a glimpse of a white tie and shirt front before he recognized the Lord President of the Council.

'Evening, sir.' He saluted.

'Evening,' the Lord President said, without looking at him. It occurred to the policeman that it was somewhat unusual for first the Foreign Secretary then the Lord President to turn up at this hour; but he did not wonder beyond that.

Entering the building, the Lord President of the Council followed the corridor to the Prime Minister's office. As he reached the screened waiting area in the ante-room, a door on the right opened and Henning appeared.

'Lord President, good evening. The Prime Minister is waiting for you. Would you come in at once?'

The Lord President's heavily hooded eyes flashed a question. But he said nothing. They went over. Without knocking, Henning opened the Prime Minister's door wide. The Prime Minister was standing a few feet inside the room with his back to the door talking to somebody. As he turned, the Lord President saw with surprise that it was the Foreign Secretary and at once his sense that something serious had occurred was confirmed.

'Come in.' The Prime Minister extended a hand. The Lord President shook it, searching his face. The door shut behind him. 'How are you, Robert?' he nodded to the Foreign Secretary. The Foreign Secretary was eighteen years younger than the Lord President, a difference which was not unmarked in the Lord President's manner.

71

'I'm sorry to get you out,' the Prime Minister said to the Lord President. 'I hope it wasn't too noticeable?'

The Lord President hunched his shoulders with a shake of his jowls. It conveyed that his departure from the Pilgrims Dinner had inevitably been noted – what could the Prime Minister expect? – but that if anybody could carry a thing like that off, it was him.

'Did the Press ask any questions?'

'I dealt with them. What has happened?'

The Prime Minister's manner and voice were perfectly controlled and calm. 'There's been a disaster to one of our nuclear submarines, *Uranus*. She has gone down inside Russian territorial waters and is lying there disabled with twenty-nine survivors. I have been telling the Secretary of State. I need your advice on what we are to do.'

The Lord President of the Council had been a party companion of the Prime Minister's for thirty-nine years. Both ambitious, both gifted with great political instinct, they had both come from smaller more radical political groups which had proved too confined for their talents and joined the party in the days when unbroken years of office stretched before it and it was picking off leading opponents by giving them posts abroad or making 'national' Ministers out of them.

The two men's paths had run parallel for years. At times, one would look like the coming Caesar, a little later, the other. Both had been Ministers in a dozen new and reshuffled governments. They had become veterans and after so many years become imbued with all the subtleties of office-holding.

Then the Prime Minister had begun to outdistance the Lord President. Nobody quite knew how it was. The process had been slow but inexorable. When he had become head of government, the Prime Minister had naturally offered the Lord President a senior post. Perhaps it was not so senior as it ought to have been; but they were intimate party colleagues.

After this, the distance between them increased. While the Prime Minister's grasp on public affairs, the party and the country deepened and strengthened, while his extraordinary political skill grew and flourished, the Lord President became

72

the ally of factions and movements and rebellious groups within the party, and even on its fringe.

It was done with enormous skill, with great virtuosity. The Lord President was a seventeenth-century courtier transmuted into modern politics. There was never a moment when he could be accused of leading a movement against the Prime Minister, far less of open betrayal. The subtlest of his opponents outside the party ranks could not claim the Lord President as guide or supporter. The voting record could not be used against him (and in fact was held up as a demonstration of the Lord President's resourcefulness).

Yet the men on the important committees, the influential back-benchers, the powerful and silent men in industry and the business world saw in the Lord President the figure they could count on when the moment came to move in and take control. He represented a thoroughgoing renewal in the establishment.

His dialectical skill was immense. With the finesse of an artist, he could, in the first few instants of talk, detect what people wanted to hear; and he showed the same penetration, the same high dexterity in playing one off against the other so as to give himself a controlling hand over all the parties to an issue. He had brought rumour-mongering to a scientific pitch and used people who questioned him to advance and work for his ideas. The ambiguous phrase, shaped for quotation, was one of his finest weapons. Political analysts quarried in these phrases for days and weeks, never sure whether they meant something commonplace or contained the portent of the new age.

Lately he had been the moving spirit behind those who maintained that the Prime Minister had made too many mistakes. He stood as the party's Hercules. He was convinced that if the Prime Minister were dropped, there would be a spontaneous movement within the party to call him in. In his hands, the party could carry the approaching election and, he would go so far as to suggest, the next.

Physically, there was nothing the Lord President looked like so much as a politician – unless it were a bloodhound. He had once been photographed with Pierre Laval and though they

73

were quite dissimilar in build or in features, a cynical French deputy had remarked that there was an unmistakable affinity of soul.

The Lord President's face was scored with deep bloodhound folds. He seemed to have entirely too much skin on his face – jowls and a long fleshy gizzard in which he gargled ecclesiastically. His face structure, with its hooded eyes and good forehead crowned by pleasantly curling grey hair, was naturally impressive. His diction was exquisite. He had one habit that distressed his friends. He constantly extruded his tongue and licked his bottom lip. There was nothing very awful in this. But the Lord President's tongue, either naturally or because of the habit, was very thick and grey and broad and long; and its constant passage over the bottom lip, which it each time covered entirely, had considerably thickened and coarsened the lip.

With his face, with his innate sense of the courtier, he could become instantly and overpoweringly solemn. The solemnity usually looked hollow and insincere. Yet the intensity with which he assumed it somehow countered people's knowledge that most of the time he was acting when he did. This was one reason why he terrified subordinates; they never knew when the folds of his face, the haggard-looking eyes and the thickened lower lip would drop into a solemn hanging mask, probably at the very moment when they felt that the Lord President was at his gayest.

Yet, of course, he had immense charm. He could be the most ingratiating of men. He was a brilliant administrator, a scholar, and had the grace and wit of a man who has always moved among the high intellects of his day. And the Prime Minister placed measureless trust in his political judgement.

Did he know of the Lord President's political infidelities? Some said he must, others that he could hardly doubt them. Some went so far as to blame the Prime Minister for sentimental weakness. Yet the fact was that the Prime Minister continued to rely on the Lord President for opinion, to lean on him in countless matters; and nobody who knew the inner workings of the government would have been entirely astonished at learning that the Prime Minister had called in the Lord President in the *Uranus* emergency.

When the Prime Minister finished his recital of the facts and had gone over his exchange with the First Sea Lord, there were a few seconds of silence.

The Lord President said, 'Are there Polaris missiles on board?'

'No. Thank God at least not that.'

'Are you sure?'

'I am confident there are not. I was told the ship would be sent without Polaris.'

'But *Uranus* is a Polaris-type submarine, is she not?' The Lord President's eyes went to the Foreign Secretary. The Foreign Secretary said, 'That is so.'

'Yes, but the missiles were not to be loaded,' the Prime Minister said. 'The Navy wanted this particular commanding officer to be used. They thought the human factor was important and since his ship was a Polaris type, it was decided to use it but to unload the missiles.'

The building of the British Polaris submarines, which had originally been intended to come into service in the late sixties, had been greatly accelerated.

The Lord President lit a cigarette. He consumed it in heavy dragging draws, as if he were eating it.

The Prime Minister went on. 'It was a secret reconnaissance. The Russians have set up these shore installations which we believe are something new – a new and very dangerous long-range anti-missile weapon. I was asked to authorize the reconnaissance after all the merits and the risks had been gone into by the Navy, the Chiefs of Staff, the Intelligence people and the Scientific Adviser. The Minister of Defence agreed that it wasn't useful to discuss it in the Defence Council. Montfalcon was all for it. I was told the services needed the information and the other implications were plain. I take full responsibility.'

Even the most unorthodox political opponents would not question the authority of Marshal of the Air Force Earl Montfalcon, the Chief of Defence Staff.

The Lord President rose from his chair. He paced down the room, turned back, stopped dead. It was the merest shade theatrical. His face was deadly solemn. 'I've no need to tell you what this means electorally if it gets out?'

It was a purely rhetorical question. The Prime Minister did not answer.

'It would not simply be a catastrophe. It would mean the eclipse of the party for a decade.'

It was true, the Prime Minister knew. They all knew too well that it was the worst moment for such a disaster. The Opposition, reinvigorated and aggressive after a period of inertia, was using every inch of political terrain to demonstrate that the government was exhausted, worn out and had fatally lost impetus. Feeling the electoral wind in its sails, it was attacking without respite and had been aided by a series of unforeseeable chances.

In particular, the Opposition's attacks in defence policy had been devastatingly well-aimed and it was obvious that they were arousing a good deal of sympathy outside Parliament. The gravamen of the charge – gravamen was a favourite word of the Lord President's – was that the government had sold out on defence to the United States and was now subjugated to the hard-bitten, youthful power group in Washington. These, the stony-faced industrial executives turned Secretaries, the professional news managers, the hatchet-men who had brought a new element of callousness and calculation into international political life, were, to the Opposition, a new generation which the Prime Minister and his party were the last people in the world equipped to deal with. The 'special relationship' with Britain was a comic piece of anachronistic sentimentality to them. Sometimes the Prime Minister felt so himself.

The Opposition's charge was a trying one to answer. The most effective answer would have been some military action in which Britain would demonstrate its independence by acting quite independently and, of course, that was a very difficult thing.

Relations with the United States had, moreover, recently been clouded by a complex series of disagreements in the

76

Caribbean, the West Indies and the former British coastal territories in the area. This had led to irritated exchanges and the hasty convening of a conference which had merely saved appearances. With exasperation the Prime Minister had heard echoes of the Opposition's criticisms from American lips and repetitions of Dean Acheson's old attacks.

Behind all this, the new American endeavour to get under-standing with Russia, worked at constantly and laboriously, sometimes eagerly, always cautiously and often in the dark, looked as if it were at last coming to something. There had, they all knew, been unusual exchanges between the President of the United States and the Soviet Premier. The American Secretary of State was having a further meeting in three weeks' time with Ostrovsky, the Soviet Foreign Minister, on 'The New Approach' as it was called. It was a moment of delicate balance.

At a point which was retrospectively now quite obvious, the Americans had come to the conclusion that, since they and the Russians both had enough nuclear weapons to destroy the world several times over, the Russians would be ready for an arrangement which would allow them to check the crippling and utterly pointless cost of manufacturing more. The Russians had responded. This was the foundation of 'The New Approach'. A full body of New Approach doctrine had now been set up. One element of the doctrine was the 'Communica-tion Principle' – the ability of one Great Power to speak directly to another Great Power. To some this looked like a rehash of the old European Socialist idea of 'the Left speaking to the Left' but these men were, of course, pooh-poohed.

The Prime Minister and his colleagues had suspected the Russians of duplicity. The Americans would not have this, would not listen. They were convinced that they knew Russian motives and intentions best. When the Prime Minister had insisted, the Americans had accused him of trying to force Britain to the forefront, to assert British influence and to arro-gate to Britain the role of a Great Power when she was no longer more than third rate. It was the old Acheson line again.

A little later, intelligence reports had come in to London of the secret installations at Chizha. They were supporting evidence of Russian deceit, of the Russian intention of playing the Americans along until they had developed this new long-range anti-missile weapon. But the last British approach had resulted in such a sharp American brush-off, the American dislike of British insistence was so pointed and undisguised, that nothing more could be done. It was then that the British decision to investigate Chizha had been taken. It could be argued that it had been a duty to the alliance. In any event, the Service Chiefs had pointed out, British security was closely and vitally involved. All these reasons had weighed in the Prime Minister's mind when he had sanctioned the mission.

The Prime Minister had managed, with great difficulty and at the price of some humiliation, to keep a foot, sometimes it seemed just a toe, in the proceedings between Americans and Russians. Apart from the main interest, British participation in 'The New Approach' would, he knew, effectively counter the Opposition onslaught. Yet it was participation which Washington barely admitted.

All these things were visibly present in the minds of the three men as they looked at each other. The Lord President said, 'It seems to me there is one obvious thing to do. Give it out that the submarine has been lost while testing in home waters.'

'But that means to condemn the men. Do nothing about them.'

The Lord President's face filled with genuine pain. 'You would be doing so in the higher interest of the country. Surely this is supremely a case of the good of the greater number.'

The Prime Minister turned his head with a low exclamation, like a groan. 'It's the cold-bloodedness of the thing.'

'You would be sacrificing twenty-nine men against – how many, who knows?'

The Foreign Secretary stood back, watching the two of them. He felt he was not expected to join in this part of the exchange.

'You have the analogy of battle,' the Lord President was saying. 'The commanding general calculates his percentage of

78

sacrifices, of his expendables. The Dieppe raid, Saint Nazaire, the German dams – good God, how many others have there been?'

'It makes it no easier to accept.'

'Are you looking for ways to make it easier, Prime Minister?' the Lord President said, and there was a slight edge to his voice.

'I ought perhaps not to be,' the Prime Minister said. 'But I am. Sixty or seventy men have gone already —' He stopped in mid-phrase. But before he could resume, the Lord President had guessed what was in his mind.

'You think there might be more alive in the ship than we know of?'

'Yes. As I now remember, the First Sea Lord said the ship's signal spoke of twenty-nine *known* survivors. That suggests that the damage has prevented them making a full count. There might be sixty men alive or more.'

'How long can they last?' the Lord President said. The Prime Minister looked at him quickly, but the Lord President had turned to the Foreign Secretary. 'Do you know?'

'In ideal conditions, for months, if not years, I believe. Everything depends on the extent of the damage. If they have twenty-nine men alive and the damage is moderate, they might last two or three weeks,' the Foreign Secretary said.

'What!' The Lord President looked aghast. He had not apparently expected this any more than the Prime Minister had. 'It is obvious we can't send rescue ships.'

'Are we to tell NATO?'

'But the Americans! It is impossible. Moreover we hinted, very carefully, at the value of reconnaissance to NATO and it was turned down.'

'Could we put up a reconnaissance plane, Prime Minister?' said the Foreign Secretary.

'No – no.'

'Good God, my boy,' the Lord President's gizzard quivered with negation. 'You mean risk another U2 affair? At this juncture? The Russians must be watching the air space there like hawks for high-flying planes. Besides, what, my dear Secretary of State (he purred placation), what could a reconnaissance plane do?'

'We should perhaps not be so entirely in the dark. Alternatively, we could send a surface craft to scout in the nearest international waters.'

'Surely the Russians would be on to it as soon as it got close enough to be any use?' the Prime Minister said. 'It's much too risky.'

'I agree. It might lead them straight to *Uranus*,' the Lord President said.

'But this is not a situation you can resolve without risk.' There was an incisive note to the Foreign Secretary's voice for the first time. 'There's going to be considerable risk if we are to get those men out.'

They stood for a moment without a word. The Lord President said, 'Do we know at what depth she is lying and if the escape chambers are working?'

'Something like forty-five fathoms,' the Prime Minister said. 'They have said nothing about escape chambers, so we assume they are workable. There is ample escape gear on board, but the commanding officer has evidently decided against using it for the moment.'

The Lord President moved away again, then pivoted. Always the actor's touch, the Foreign Secretary thought. 'Then there must be a decision at once.'

'You mean they will start to escape?' the Prime Minister said.

'And be picked up by the Russians. It seems inevitable.'

'Lord President, what is in your mind?'

The Lord President's tone was almost hortatory. 'Do they know, these men, do they realize what may depend on them – on their discipline, on their elevation of mind, in a moment of crisis, on their spirit of sacrifice?'

'You are proposing that we ask them to commit suicide?' the Prime Minister said. 'To stay in the submarine when they have the chance to escape?'

'To do their duty in the highest sense,' the Lord President

said. He had lifted his chin and his face was set proudly in its heavy lines.

'Do you imagine those men sitting there, looking at the escape gear and letting death overtake them on the strength of an appeal, an order? It would be – it would be barbaric – it —'

'It would be heroic.'

'Asking too much – too much!'

'Are you sure, Prime Minister, that you are not under-estimating the calibre of these men?' It was hollow – pure acting, the Foreign Secretary thought again. Yet in spite of himself he admired and was impressed. He said, 'We don't know if the Captain has complete control of the situation. He may not be able to stop escapes. They are relatively close in. If there is a chance of reaching the Russian coast, somebody is bound to try. I remember a German sailor, sunk in a U-boat during the war in the Persian Gulf, who swam twenty-odd miles – the equivalent of a cross-Channel swim – towing a wounded officer part of the way; and he got ashore.'

The Lord President said, 'But in these cold Russian waters? It is almost the Arctic.'

There was an abrupt break, as if they all realized with a shock where the exchange was heading. The Prime Minister faced the Lord President. 'What are we to do?'

'I think there's no doubt; they must be sacrificed. I say it with deep regret. We should announce that the submarine has been lost with all hands on exercises in the Atlantic or some-where similar.'

'But how will that serve?' the Prime Minister said. 'The Russians may pick up a survivor an hour after our announce-ment. They may locate the submarine from an oil-slick or debris. We should be worse off than ever.'

'Then we should have to bluff coldly.' The Lord President's expression cleared. He was almost buoyant. He looked, the Foreign Secretary thought, formidably skilful. If it came to bluff, he would be unapproachable. 'We should have to speak of lost contact, of trouble with the ship on trials – there would be twenty plausible reasons. Perhaps we would have to go

81

further.' The inference was clear.

'Further?' the Prime Minister said. 'Disown the men whom we have sacrificed? Castigate them?'

'There are no conditions to the ideal of service. These men would not be the first unsung heroes.'

'But the lies it would entail, the monstrous deception! – if it were successful.'

'Even at the cost of great tension with the Russians, it would give us time, it would get us out of this present extremely ugly situation.'

'And if, as the Secretary of State says, the Captain does not control the situation and can't prevent the men escaping?'

'Prime Minister, you are asking for an ideal solution. And there is none. Whatever is done, moreover, must be done with utmost speed.'

The Prime Minister looked at him with haggard eyes.

CHAPTER SEVEN

KIRBY, THE RADIO operator who was keeping the watch with Groves, had picked up a home news bulletin broadcast for shipping and transcribed it. Fivesman, the Coxswain, was nearly at the end of reading it aloud in the wardroom.

'Five payroll bandits held up a van carrying builders' wages in Nottingham today and got away with eleven thousand pounds. At Bow Street, London, Magistrates' Court, a man was fined forty shillings or a month's jail for creating a public nuisance by letting a box of African red ants loose in the linger-ee, all right, the longzheree department of a West End store. Asked his motive, accused said, "I 'ad a dream." Cricket results Kent four hundred and one all out, Sussex seventy-three for two. Gloucester one hundred and eleven for nine declared. All other matches rain stopped play. Polo: Cowdray Gold Cup won by Windsor Park after extra time. The match con-cluded in a downpour.'

He finished. 'Well chums, who cares, now we got the polo results, eh? Apart from that, everything looks like business as usual, don't it? Rain stops play.' He chuckled and tossed the sheet on to the table.

'Where you goin' for your summer holidays, Chief?'

'He always goes to the Continong, don't you, Chief? Follow the longzheree at Ostend.'

Jason looked round the men at the table, the others standing or squatting.

Nobody had spoken of what was in all their minds – that the bulletin had said nothing about a submarine disaster. Yet it was an item no ship's news sheet would miss if it were given out. He wished he had seen the sheet first. Would he have to stop Kirby taking the bulletins down? But that would not stop the news circulating that there was silence about them in the world above.

He got up. 'Thank you, lads. We'll have a return uckers tomorrow. Good night.'

'Good night, sir.'

In the control room, Farrell and Hoyle were sprawled on the deck, talking together in low voices. Monkhouse was in one of the steersmen's seats and Lieutenant Bailey lurched sideways asleep in the other. Farrell and Hoyle did not look up.

Jason swung up the ladder to the bridge. He needed a cigarette but he had rationed the men to one each a day to check air pollution and he wasn't going to exceed it himself.

He cleared the chart table and hoisted himself up on it. He sat with his back against the bulkhead, legs extended. He switched off the emergency light. Only the dim glow from the control room below illuminated the compartment.

He felt embittered and full of doubts. The disaster was being hushed up. Yet there was a silent expectation among the men that something would be done. How could it be otherwise? It was bound up with their loyalty to the service, since it was implicit that the service would be loyal to them. Otherwise, service became complete abnegation. They all knew there were moments when it must come to that and no less. But to accept this complete negation was so hard! You needed an assertion to get men to die like this. A fighting action against the enemy was one thing. But what were they to die for now? For the sake of secrecy? For the sake of silence?

He was suddenly shaken. It was the sort of thing French officers fighting in Indo-China and Algeria had kept on asking themselves; what are we being asked to die for? To him, at a distance, it had seemed another world in which you would ask such a question. He had felt aloof and safe from it. They had blamed 'the politicians', as if the politicians were a separate race.

Yet wasn't he asking it now? Could you separate their situation neatly, surgically, from the politicians' world? How many Englishmen now would smile at the naivety of such a question!

The incongruously comic buzz of somebody playing on a comb came up from below. He jumped down to the deck. He felt tormentedly that he had drifted into confusion of mind. The issue was plain. They had failed on a service mission and they could not be saved because of the political consequences. All you died for in war, after all, were political consequences. Yet surely there must be a gesture from home to help them? Even if it only kept up some sort of comforting illusion until they no longer had the energy to get out of the submarine.

He sat on the stool brooding. The dark surroundings of the compartment intermingled with his thoughts and the sounds from the ship, the ticking of the clock, voices, footsteps passing to and fro.

An hour later, Groves came up with a signal. Jason took out the books and deciphered it alone. He sat reading the text on the pink pad.

Uranus from Ministry of Defence. You will not repeat not transmit further. Strict silence is to be kept. Appropriate measures are being taken regarding you. Be in good heart.

He raised his head. He was aware of a new sound. It came from aft, an irregular tapping sound. Something was moving along the hull of the submarine outside.

Petty Officer Grimble swam up to the dark of consciousness. For a second or two, lying with his eyes open, he had the impression of spinning in emptiness, going faster and faster. The impression was caused by the total darkness around him and his endeavours to situate himself at some point of time and space. Somewhere – he did not distinguish it as his leg yet – he was feeling great pain. Then everything came back. He felt the steel deck under him. He sensed the invisible space of the compartment around him. Pain burned up his leg. He felt very thirsty.

Suddenly he was sure he was the only survivor, the last man alive in the submarine. Perhaps the others had all escaped and forgotten him? He raised himself; but the pain in his leg made him flinch sideways against the wheel of the hatch. He did not want to touch his leg. He could feel the torn dungarees clinging stickily to it.

He lay staring into the dark. Drops of water were falling at intervals somewhere. He ran his hand over the deck plating round him. It was dry. Then it came to him that since he was in an enclosed space, there must be watertight bulkheads all round and watertight doors shut. He shouted out. Nobody answered.

Grimble wanted to cry. He was pressing his head to his chest to control the impulse. He grasped the hatch wheel and pulled himself to a sitting position. He must find a light.

He gave himself a moment, turned on to his good side. Using his hands, he dragged himself over the deck. The compartment was in complete darkness. His shoulder bumped into something. He reached up and ran his hands over a piece of machinery, probably a small turbine; but he couldn't situate it.

He dragged himself past it and touched a wire guard. Reaching up, he found a cluster of gauges, cocks and piping. He knew he had to get to his feet to find the emergency lights. Gripping a gauge, he hauled himself to a standing position on his good leg. The sweat was out all over his body.

He groped along the bulkhead and found a light. He looked round with some apprehension; he had thought of seeing bodies in the compartment, but he was alone. He was facing aft. Almost immediately in front of him was the thwartships bulkhead separating him from the next compartment. The watertight door was shut and clipped over.

God Almighty, Grimble said to himself, let there be somebody there. He swung himself over to it and, gripping the upper clip, he thumped on the door with his fist. He felt how punily ineffective his flesh was against the steel and shouted out, 'Open up, boys! Open up. This is Grimble. I can't make it. Open up!'

There was no answer. He put his face close to the door and yelled again. Still no answer.

He tried to pull the clip back; but the effort sent hot rods of pain down his leg and he couldn't continue. He cast round for some implement. There was an oil-can ten feet away. He was breathing hard.

He worked his way round to the oil-can, picked it up – it was nearly empty – and returned to the door. He hammered the can on the steel door until he was breathess. It sounded feeble too. He hung there, grasping the clip. Nothing happened. There must be somebody behind the door – unless they were dead.

Quickly and overwhelmingly, the conviction came on him that whoever was there was dead. He let go the clip. He looked round at the other door at the far end of the compartment. He was shaking; he had an appalling fear of finding the compartment there flooded and unresponsive too. All at once he thought of the intercom phone. As quickly as he could, he moved round to it. He stood for a moment with the instrument in his hand, getting his nerve back. Then he rang Bridge. There was no reply. Control room. No reply. 'Hello...? hello...? Jesus bloody Christ, where you all gone?' He pressed all the buttons. Nobody answered.

Grimble hung up. He looked towards the far door. He began to move towards it. The light dimmed, he became dizzy, twisted round in his attempt to save himself and fell to the deck.

His tongue and palate were adhering like dried glue and sandpaper. He opened his eyes. He did not know if he had been lying there five minutes or five hours.

He tried to work a little saliva into his mouth. He could not hear the falling drops any more. His head ached and he felt his injured leg warm and sticky; it had evidently been bleeding again.

After a moment he stirred painfully. He was lying facing the after watertight door. As he stared at it, a trick of self-projection seemed to operate in him. He saw himself behind the door, lying helpless, unable to reply to the knocking on the other side. Perhaps somebody was there. Yet if the compartment were flooded and he managed to open the door, he would never get it shut again against the pressure of water.

He lay back. Presently he turned his head and caught a glint of steel on the deck alongside the machine housing. It was a heavy double-ended spanner, about two feet long. Grimble turned on his side and pulled it out. He crawled over to the door, lay down alongside it and, wielding the spanner with both hands, swung it against the door with all the strength he had. Gaspingly between blows, he stopped. Metallic raps were coming from the other side. His inner self poured out in gratitude. At an infinite distance, he seemed to hear a shout. He yelled back, hit again with the spanner. More blows from the other side.

Grimble grasped the bottom clip and pulled on it. It gave a little. The next moment, he felt it sharply released from the other side, then the top clip was undone.

He shoved himself back. The door opened an inch or two. He could see an arm and bare shoulder against it, a section of face in the gap. Then it swung wide and Beale came in. Grimble looked up with uncontrollable relief.

'Who is it?' Beale peered forward at Grimble's blackened face. 'Lofty! Who's in here? Ain't making water, are you?'

'You didn't answer. I been yelling like mad, banging on that door.'

'I thought I heard something faint. I couldn't tell what . . . I . . . Who you got with you? Where's the others?' Beale stepped quickly past him into the compartment, looking round.

Grimble turned, watching him, feeling, behind his relief, a curious apprehension.

CHAPTER EIGHT

THE LIGHT IN the Cabinet Room at 10 Downing Street
was fading. It was not quite dusk but nobody had switched on
the lights. The last glow from the windows made some things
in the room stand out with unusual clarity – the outline of the
fireplace, the columns, the papers on the table.

The Prime Minister was sitting in his customary place at
the centre of the table. The Defence Minister was at his right;
on the other side was the Lord President, then the Foreign
Secretary and, opposite him, Air Marshal the Earl Mont-
falcon, Chief of the Defence Staff. The First Secretary of
State sat next to the Foreign Secretary facing the First Sea
Lord; the last two seats were occupied by the Chief of the
General Staff and the Chief of the Air Staff.

This was a restricted version of the Committee on Defence
and Oversea Policy. The full Committee included other
Ministers such as the Chancellor of the Exchequer and the
Home Secretary; but the practice had grown up of using this
smaller group when matters short of long-term policy were
being discussed.

The setting of the famous room seemed to heighten the
sense of occasion. Each place at the table had before it a black
leather blotter embossed in gilt with the Sovereign's initials
and the words 'Cabinet Room First Lord'. Disposed at intervals over the green-baize cloth were heavy glass inkwells,
glass ashtrays, carafes and tumblers, racks of writing paper,
four slender Georgian candlesticks. At the window end, in
addition, was the heavy silver dish-like shape of the Pitt
candlestick, kept there traditionally. No sound came from outside.

The nine men had been at the table for an hour. They
nevertheless sat attentively, even tensely, leaning forward,
their heads turning as one, then another spoke. Only the Lord

President sat hunched and brooding, his eyes following the discussion. Charts of the area in which the submarine was lying were among the papers on the table. Some of the Ministers had brought files. The Foreign Secretary was taking notes of what was said.

Montfalcon was speaking. He was a man with a hawk-like face (which was supposed to be one reason for his choice of title) – a high thin aquiline nose, flat planes of cheeks and hard eyes. The sparseness of his eyebrows added to the effect of coldness. He spoke with his chin up and the pride of his bearing made even the First Sea Lord look a man of ordinary size. When he had finished, the Prime Minister said, 'It is vital to know if it is a Russian attack. Has the ship been torpedoed; is it a minefield or is there some system of defence we know nothing about?'

The First Sea Lord said, 'It is impossible to tell. The signal implies that they don't know themselves.'

There was a knock on the door and Henning came in. He hesitated a second, seeing the room in semi-gloom, then switched on the light. The men at the table stirred in the sudden brightness.

Henning bent to the Prime Minister's ear and said a few words, placing a paper before him. The Prime Minister's face clouded. A spasm of impatience seemed to catch him; he quickly took up the paper, nodding to Henning. 'Thank you.'

As he read, Montfalcon leaned forward and spoke across the table to the First Secretary of State. Listening, the First Secretary took off his rimless glasses and began polishing them with a silk handkerchief. Without them, his pale hairless face under the tight fuzz of hair (which visiting foreigners often took for a wig) looked curiously unfurnished.

The First Secretary had made a million in the City at thirty and, at one time, had been the party's golden boy. But there was a side to him that was bored. The one thing that held his mind was finance and he could do all he wanted with that in an hour a day. He had gone into politics in the hope of a thrill from high office but hadn't found it. Things came too easily to him. He turned from one subject to another but remained bored. He was still young but knew with inner conviction that he was not going to live long; he was quite unmoved by the knowledge and his life was strangely taut and empty.

The Prime Minister looked up. 'They have made another signal. It gives the position and says "Request urgent assistance to save survivors." They were told not to break radio silence, were they not, First Sea Lord?'

'Yes,' the First Sea Lord said.

The Prime Minister passed the signal to him.

'Isn't that suspicious?' the Defence Minister said. 'Would they disregard a specific order like that?' The First Sea Lord bent over a chart, marking the position as the others passed the signal round.

'The position is five miles from the coast, off Chizha,' the First Sea Lord said. 'Russian territorial waters extend twelve miles from the coast. *Uranus* is seven miles inside.'

There was silence at the table. It was as if they had hoped up to that moment that it would not be quite so close.

'The Russians could have put it out,' the Foreign Secretary said. 'It doesn't seem like them, I must say. It doesn't strike me as something they would do.'

The First Sea Lord shook his head. 'No, no. I think we can disregard that possibility. It would mean they had captured the cipher and the last thing they'd do if they had would be to let us know they'd got it by sending this signal. Too valuable to them.'

'On the other hand, the signal might be the indication that the Russians have a clue to the submarine being in the area and are trying to locate it.'

'Then what assistance could the commanding officer expect from us?' the Lord President put in tartly.

'With respect, Lord President, that's not yet the point,' the First Secretary said. The Lord President flashed him a glance but said nothing.

'It comes to this,' the Prime Minister said. 'The Russians may have sunk the submarine or located her independently. If so, they are keeping mum, playing their own game and holding it over our heads. Either they are going to use it for political blackmail or they are going to make the disclosure anyway and are going to choose the moment to make it as devastating as possible, just as they did with the U2. None of us needs reminding of the way they silently let the Summit meeting in Paris build up, knowing they were going to blow it sky high with the U2 . . . those damnable scenes afterwards.'

He looked round the table. There were grim lips.

The Foreign Secretary took a sheet from the file in front of him. 'I have had the Russian statement about foreign submarines looked up. It was put out by Tass six weeks ago and mentions "authorized circles" but almost certainly comes from Kruschev himself. It is datelined Moscow.' He read out ' "Authorized circles stated tonight that foreign submarines have been sneaking close to Soviet shores on underwater manoeuvres and observations with the object of reconnaissance".' The Foreign Secretary looked up. 'That's purely defensive, of course, protective; the Americans have kept well off.' He resumed reading: ' "In conformity with international law and according to the legislation of the USSR, foreign submarines can enter Soviet territorial waters only by permission of the USSR government and must be on the surface while in these waters. The USSR government has instructed the USSR Ministry of Defence to destroy foreign submarines discovered in Soviet territorial waters and will consider any such intrusion as aggressively designed".'

The Foreign Secretary put the paper back into the file. A moment's silence followed.

The Lord President drew heavily on his cigarette. The smoke emerged on his breath as he spoke. 'Can you imagine the effect on the meeting with the Americans and ourselves in Moscow if Kruschev suddenly brings this out?' He paused and they all waited for him to go on. The Defence Minister noticed that the fingers of the Lord President's right hand were stained with nicotine.

'If they are keeping it up their sleeves it will be far worse for us to say nothing – far worse. It will be letting them have the full benefit of the disclosure. The wreckage they will cause

92

will be far more widespread. I urge upon the Prime Minister and the Committee that something be said without delay. We must make an announcement. I suggest that we announce an accidental disaster.'

He turned to the First Sea Lord. 'Admiral, is there anything on which we could base a plausible statement of accident with a ship of this type at this interval after her trials? If so, what sort of accident?'

The First Sea Lord's glance narrowed.

'If you were answering a Court of Inquiry?' the Lord President said.

'A Court of Inquiry? Do you suggest, Lord President, that officers would be asked to fabricate evidence for a Court —'

'*Find* evidence, First Sea Lord. The Court would, in any case, be sitting *in camera*.' The Lord President was at his smoothest. The folds of his face lifted for a second in a humourless smile. It made the First Secretary think of a curtain being twitched up, then dropped; entirely meaningless.

'Come, come, Admiral. I admire your scrupulousness. I hope I share it,' the Lord President went on. 'But we are going to be obliged to make an extremely convincing demonstration not only to the Russians but to public opinion if we are not to suffer something far more serious.' His voice had dropped to a deep baying and his face was solemn.

The First Sea Lord was looking at him steadily. His face had coloured. None of them failed to notice his brief struggle to control himself.

The Prime Minister broke in. His tone seemed deliberately considerate. 'Had the ship any special difficulties, First Sea Lord? On trials for instance? If it comes to it, and we have to, what sort of case could be made out for an accident?'

The First Sea Lord obviously disliked this whole line. Nevertheless, he sifted through the papers in front of him. 'We had trouble with the sodium cycle superheating system in the reactor power unit.'

'Could that be the cause of the ship's now being disabled?'

'I think not. I would have to get an expert view but it seems unlikely.'

'But it is conceivable?'

'Yes. Conceivable.'

'Would you explain a little further, First Sea Lord?' the Lord President said, all conciliation.

'*Uranus* is powered by what is known as SIR or Submarine Intermediate Reactor. This uses liquid sodium metal as the heat-exchange agent in the atomic reactor power unit. Briefly, the liquid sodium is heated by the fission process in the reactor core and then passes through pipes into a "boiler" or heat exchanger where it converts water into steam. The steam is then used to drive turbines geared to the submarine's propeller shafts.'

'That is not the same system as we used in *Dreadnought* and *Valiant*, I believe?'

'No, Prime Minister. The hunter-killers are powered by STR or Submarine Thermal Reactor.'

Montfalcon said, 'The sodium, in other words, transfers the heat generated by the atomic fission to the boiler which turns it into steam?'

'That is so. The sodium gave us a lot of trouble with corrosion in the tubes. The ship was working on reduced power for some time.'

'Why use sodium at all?' the Prime Minister asked.

'Well, sir, it boils only at extremely high temperatures, which means that we need not pressurize the cooler system. Sodium is an excellent heat conductor. If its oxygen content is low, it does not, in principle, corrode steels at operating temperatures. This, as I say, was one of our troubles. It's a good electrical conductor and you can therefore circulate it by a magnetic pump which has no moving parts. Then again, the intermediate spectrum neutrons in the SIR mean that you have a wider choice of structural materials for the reactor core. For instance, we use stainless steel in *Uranus*. This is because conventional metals don't readily absorb high-energy neutrons. The neutrons in *Uranus*'s reactor give something like twenty times the energy the thermal neutrons in *Dreadnought*'s reactor. All these are adequate reasons for using sodium.'

Nobody spoke for a moment. Abruptly, the First Secretary

said, 'We are surely drifting from the point. Accident or not, the Russians have either located the submarine or will very soon do so and we must now provide for that situation.'

The Prime Minister caught Montfalcon's eye. He said, 'We will break for ten minutes.'

There was general movement and pushing back of chairs. They all rose. The First Sea Lord, the Foreign Secretary and the Lord President went out of the room. Henning came in and spoke to the Prime Minister; and then, at a glance from the Prime Minister, Montfalcon came over. They went to the far side of the room and stood there apart, speaking in quiet voices.

The Prime Minister took a cigarette from his case and lighted it. He looked tired but completely relaxed and in control of himself. 'This may be a very serious situation, John. I don't think we can afford to be off our guard.'

'Do you mean they may attack us?'

'My feeling is they won't. Yet we can't be sure and we dare not take a chance. Finding the submarine, especially in that situation off one of their most secret installations, is going to be a very great shock to them. They were immensely shaken by the U2 flights. Kruschev had to behave as he did or he wouldn't have lasted another three months. Yet those were comparatively easy days. Now, of course, he is in an immeasurably more difficult situation.

'The present power struggle in the Kremlin is a tremendous thing. If Kruschev makes one inadequate move, Derzhavin and the new group will obliterate him. They are waiting to pounce and they have very powerful support indeed – the army and air force and much of the Party. It is one of the frightful risks we all run; we are dealing with these men's personal status. There are circumstances where Kruschev could act reasonably only at the immediate cost of his political life. He couldn't afford this penetration of Soviet territorial waters all this length of time after the U2 and after that statement the Secretary of State read out without some strong reaction. And we don't know what the anger and dismay of the moment might set off. A limited attack on Portland? On some other base? We can't tell. What I mean, John, is that this could be the threshold.'

Montfalcon nodded. His cold grey eyes held the Prime Minister's unflinchingly. He said, 'There are no reports from our radar or from NATO of any unusual Russian air activity.'

'No. I know. In some ways it is even more disquieting. It could mean surprise attack. Everything is going to happen with appalling suddenness if it does happen. We shall only have those four and a half minutes. Do you think we should go to first readiness?'

Montfalcon said, 'Yes. I think we should. We must be in a defensive posture.'

'You have a contingency plan ready?'

'Yes.'

In a few moments, they both knew, once the order was given, the code word passed over the Ministry of Defence's Telex system, hundreds of aircraft crews would be alerted. In bases and camps and defence sites and ports up and down the country, men would move to a plan which a few had practised in exercise and others had scarcely heard of or heard of not at all.

The V-bombers, their refuelling tankers and the TSR 2s would take off from their bases in East Anglia. The Bloodhound sites would be fully manned. The warships would recall crews ashore and those with steam up would put to sea. No ship could raise steam in four and a half minutes but those without it would hope for the best and clear port as soon as possible.

All over England, tanks and mobile guns and army radio vans would roll out of depots and scatter in small groups among the hedgerows. The fuel tankers for the armour – a high priority nuclear target for an enemy – would be dispersed with special rapidity.

The country's permanent stand-by troops would be sent by stand-by headquarters to prepared destinations. In barracks and camps and sidings, transport would begin to assemble, for most of the emergency operations prepared consisted in moving people to the right places in the right order. Joint Signals

and Joint Movements would be combining in calling up and assembling the Emergency Reserve of technicians for manning service communications and suchlike which were not normally kept at full strength.

Ships halfway across the Atlantic would be turned back. Shipping in the Baltic and round the Norwegian coast would be summoned home. Requisitioning calls would go out to the country's air lines and checks made on the whereabouts of all aircraft flying.

Each Ministry of the government would begin to undertake the task assigned to it to meet the emergency.

Montfalcon crossed to where the Chief of the General Staff and the Chief of Air Staff were talking and all three quickly left the room.

The Prime Minister looked round and beckoned to the Defence Minister. In a few phrases, he told him of the decision to go to the first degree of readiness. The Defence Minister listened in silence. It was clear that he was deeply shocked.

'It is going to be general knowledge very quickly; and as soon as the Russians know they are surely going to find it confirmation of hostility on our part. It is going to look to them as if *Uranus* really intended launching missiles at them.'

'As you heard, the ship is not carrying missiles.'

'Then they are quite likely to believe that she has ditched them – got rid of them – according to some security procedure.'

'I don't see how we can help that.' He looked round again. 'The Foreign Secretary is not here. We are keeping a close monitoring watch on Soviet broadcasts, are we not?'

'Yes. So far there has been no sign that they know about the submarine. But of course that means nothing.'

'Has there been any warning of Russian activity from the Americans, from Omaha, SAC or Norad?'

'Nothing yet.'

But that was not conclusive, the Prime Minister knew.

The Lord President came in talking earnestly with the Foreign Secretary. The Prime Minister noted it with disquiet.

He took his seat. 'Let us resume,' he said. Briefly, in a quiet

97

voice, he announced that he had given the alert order. There was a sudden change in the atmosphere at the table.

'But good God – it can't come to this.' The Lord President's face was grey. His tongue emerged and passed slowly over his lower lip. For a few seconds he looked old. Then he seemed to make an effort over himself and sat up with his former assurance.

He raised a hand. 'I would like to speak. I must say this to the Prime Minister, with all deference but also in full responsibility and with all the gravity I can as a Minister of the Crown. We have, under our agreement with the United States, a moral obligation to inform the President about our preparations to meet attack. Whatever the circumstances – unless the course I urge is taken – we must, unavoidably, inform the United States. It is inherent for one thing in the terms of the Alliance and in our special understanding of the Nassau agreement according to the interpretation which we discussed in Washington after the agreement was reached.'

'We are not bound to inform the President if we are simply *preparing* for defence,' the Prime Minister said.

'It happens that our joint contingency planning has not covered the particular circumstances we now find ourselves in,' the Lord President said. 'But if we must go to the length of alerting the V-bombers and preparing to make even a limited, a tactical, reply to attack, we are bound to tell the President of the United States. We are morally bound to inform him now, at this instant, even as the Chiefs of Staff put the preparations into motion. We have that obligation as soon as we conceive the danger of attack on us to exist, since that danger may, by escalation, build up immediately into a direct danger to the United States.

'All the American bases here, not merely Holy Loch, are certainly high up on the Russian target list and the Russians will go for them very early on in any escalated attack. For this reason alone, it would be inconceivable not to inform the United States.

'But even if the Russians do not intend to attack us in the next hours or minutes, we cannot afford not to inform the

United States. If the Russians announce the capture of the submarine and violation of their territorial waters while we are silent, there is going to be a – a convulsion in America! Suez will be nothing to it! We shall have brought the United States within the risk of war without breathing a word to them. It would be catastrophic! It would be the end of a British voice in the Atlantic Alliance. It would be the end of any shadow of British influence in America for decades – generations!

'All this is manifest. And it is why, Prime Minister, I press upon you, I urge upon you and the Committee most earnestly that the only course open to us is to feint.'

'How?' The Prime Minister was leaning forward in his chair. He had followed the Lord President closely.

'We must cold-bloodedly, here and now, simulate an accident. We must send rescue ships and aircraft out into the North Sea, somewhere off the northern coast of Norway, in international waters. We must put all the machinery of a genuine submarine disaster into motion – broadcasts to shipping, new bulletins, press conferences and so forth. All the time, of course, and repeatedly, we should stress that the submarine was carrying out prolonged submerged tests. We should refer to the trouble with the sodium system which the First Sea Lord has told us about, and the navigating gear. We should be searching for the submarine and failing to find her.'

'And there would be a Court of Inquiry?' the Defence Minister said.

'It would be essential! Essential. One of its high important purposes would be to establish that there had been trouble with the ship's gyro compass and other navigating equipment.'

'And when the Russians came across *Uranus* or picked up survivors?' the Defence Minister said.

'The heat would be off,' the Lord President said, leaning forward. He looked at his most formidable. 'Don't you see that? It would be another situation. There would be doubt, suspicion, disbelief – oh! profound disbelief – but the danger would have been taken out of the situation.'

The Prime Minister looked on the rack. 'The lies – a system of carefully articulated lies – I – it couldn't be done.'

'It is done daily in war, Prime Minister,' the Lord President said. 'Is it not justifiable to prevent war?'

The First Secretary said, 'The searches for a missing nuclear submarine would go on for weeks, even months.'

'We should have to carry the thing through convincingly. Or not begin,' the Lord President said acidly.

'I agree with the Lord President,' the Foreign Secretary said. Everybody looked at him.

At the same moment, the First Sea Lord and the Chief of the General Staff came in together and resumed their places. The First Secretary leaned forward and quietly and briefly summarized what had passed in their absence. The First Lord's expression tensed.

'We must assume the Russians will locate the submarine,' the Defence Minister said. 'And when they find the gyro compass in good order they will expose us.'

The Lord President allowed himself a sardonic smile. It gave him the extraordinarily amusing and witty and ravaged look that appealed so much to women. The Lord President had had love-affairs with some of the most brilliant women of the day and had a Stendhalian reputation.

'Come, come, Minister. We know how the Russians are constantly faking evidence. They would never be believed. We should carry it off without any trouble. In any event, the submarine has reported extensive damage and there is nothing to show they would ever be able to establish what went wrong.'

The Prime Minister laid his hands, palms down, on the table. He was calm but plainly worked on by deep feelings. 'Lord President, I feel the government cannot go along on those lines. I could not recommend it to the sovereign.'

'Then you must inform the President of the United States.' There was finality in the Lord President's tone. He took a cigarette from his case and lit it with a quick gesture. But as the Prime Minister was about to speak again, he intervened. 'Are you sure, Prime Minister, that there is no American equipment in *Uranus*?'

'What do you mean?'

'You remember that in Newport last year the President agreed under pressure to our having certain items of equipment on his own authority, that is without direct Congressional approval, until we developed our own. As I remember, we pressed for those items and got them.'

The Prime Minister's eyes went to the First Sea Lord. There was agonized inquiry in them. The First Sea Lord said, 'Yes, that is so.'

The Lord President at once seemed to sense the Admiral's resistance. 'Are they in *Uranus*, First Sea Lord?'

The First Sea Lord hesitated, then nodded.

'What are they?' the Lord President said.

'There is the hypersensitive new sonar which goes far beyond anything known before. There is also a very sophisticated decoy and a navigational scope; and, of course, Subroc. The one she has is an advanced new version of the old long-range American submarine rocket which is fired submerged, breaks out into the air for a long distance and then dives again for a homing attack.'

The Lord President looked round the table. 'Ministers will need to make no effort to imagine the effect if the Americans were to believe that this material had been heedlessly jeopardized. If the Russians announce that they have captured it first, it will be infinitely worse. For these additional reasons, I urge that we do as I suggest.'

The Foreign Secretary said, 'I support the Lord President. It seems to me there are fewer risks in what he proposes than in the alternatives. I see an extremely dangerous possibility – that the Russians may capture the submarine and survivors, announce it and *then* attack us, at the very moment when the Americans are most furious with us.'

This was the situation they had faced in theory many times. Yet they had never seen it precisely like this. There was a terrible sense of inadequacy in all their minds. They knew that the threat of a Russian attack on the British Isles had always been foreseen in conjunction with a threatened American attack on Russia. The very hope of survival in Britain rested on the assumption that Britain would not be alone at that

101

dreadful moment – on the assumption that it was inconceivable for Russia to attack Britain alone, since behind Britain stood the immense nuclear striking power of the United States. The whole system had been worked out on that assumption and everything else was bound up with it. All the most exhaustive contingency planning had been done on that basis – combinations of circumstances and permutations of combinations. The contingency plan providing for the defence of Britain alone was away down the list; and, low as it was, was considered scarcely more than a bit of fantasy.

Of course there had been many statements about the 'independent British deterrent'. But no one had seriously imagined its being lifted against Russia independently of the United States – that is, without the massive and instant support of the American Atlases, Titans, Minutemen, bombers, Polaris submarines with all their thousands of thermonuclear megatons.

The British V-bombers now being made ready, the Tactical Strike and Reconnaissance 2s – only a few of them still – all these had limited targets in Russia. The many others targets in Russia, without which a nuclear strike against Russia would be pointless, were allocated to the American missiles, bombers and submarines. The radar warning system was partly, even largely, in American hands.

The Russians knew all this. The Russians knew the Americans knew it. The Russians knew, or had a strong conviction, that the United States would not, whatever happened, immediately and unconditionally throw everything in to defend Britain. An earlier Foreign Secretary had admitted as much in the House of Commons: '... To suppose that the United States will, in all circumstances, protect Britain represents a security risk that Her Majesty's Government cannot take ...' Yet it had taken that risk.

The Russians knew that the United States would, at the least, hesitate to come to Britain's help in circumstances like the present – a purely British responsibility, a case in which Britain would, in American eyes, be blameworthy and reprehensible. The American President could not be expected to gamble with the existence of the United States in such circumstances.

This, when it came to it, was what the Gaullists and men on the Continent had said all along; the bomb had changed the very meaning of alliances. There were circumstances in which military alliances simply would not operate any longer. Perhaps these circumstances were only few – but they were there.

If it was barely credible that an American government would risk annihilation to safeguard its supreme national interests, these men on the Continent had argued, it was hard to believe that they would run equivalent risks for another country, even an ally. Could the American nation now be expected to immolate itself because the British government had misjudged, had fallen victim to a mischance? The question scarcely bore asking.

Then Britain, with her 'independent nuclear deterrent', was alone? What would be the answer to a tactical Russian punitive attack on British shipping or British ports? On Birmingham or Coventry? To send the British V-bombers to try to bomb Russian ports in turn, while the teletypes chattered between London and Washington and thousands of miles away the American missiles rose out of their silos and the bombers and fighters of SAC and Norad took to the air in readiness *to defend America* – and, in a matter of minutes after the first exchanges the attack was escalating and Russian rockets were wiping the British Isles off the map?

Alone, Britain's 'independent deterrent' would not deter. And it was grotesque to think of Britain striking first. But then it meant 'independence' except at the very moment when it came to the country's life or death. That was what it *did* mean. Worse, if the Americans suspected some impending independent British nuclear action – since *independent* could only mean one they had not approved of beforehand – they would come down with both feet against it.

The threat of nuclear retaliation was credible between Russia and America because, after the first exchanges – aimed at each other's towns – each country would still have power to strike at the other. But not so Britain. Russia would only need to strike once to annihilate Britain entirely. A British nuclear strike against Russia would probably be mortal – to Britain. It would be like the sting of a bee which dies through stinging.

Supposing we reckoned that three or four V-bombers would get through. Could Britain deter Russia by threatening to bombard three or four Russian towns? No. Compared to the Russian threat which meant the obliteration of the whole of British territory at one blow, a British threat to annihilate three or four Russian towns would not carry any weight. It would be without conviction – an empty threat. It would no longer be retaliation, because after this first blow, there would be nothing left of Britain. To use the V-bombers alóne would be risking national suicide. The Russians would never be convinced that we would risk national suicide for the sake of destroying four or five Russian towns. The only way we could make the Russians believe we meant business would be to strike first. That we could not do – and even if we did, it would none the less probably mean the end of Britain.

Yet the country must defend itself, it must use what weapons it had to meet an attack; and the best of these were the bombers.

All of them at the table had these thoughts in their minds.

The First Secretary said, 'How do we know that the Russians haven't picked up some of the crew whom the Captain either knows nothing about or believes are dead and are at this moment preparing them for a mammoth trial complete with "confessions" and the rest?'

'We don't,' the Lord President snapped, 'and, since we can't find out, it's a waste of time to speculate on it. The realities are urgent enough.'

The Foreign Secretary said, 'In any event, the Russians are bound to make it look as black as they can. They will claim that they detected the ship, disarmed her and so forth – which may be true for all we know. With a few mocked-up Polaris missiles, they could credibly paint it as premeditated aggression.'

An involuntary exclamation escaped the Prime Minister.

'That is another reason why,' the Foreign Secretary went

on, 'I believe the Lord President is right and we must quickly announce that the ship has been lost.'

With inner alarm, the Prime Minister noticed the expression on the Defence Minister's face; he was suddenly looking convinced by what the Foreign Secretary had said.

The Chief of the General Staff said, 'Bodies and debris have surely risen to the surface by now?' They all looked at the First Sea Lord.

'Very likely,' the First Sea Lord said.

'That would tend to show that the Russians know she's there, would it not?' the Prime Minister said.

Quickly the Foreign Secretary put in, 'And if they haven't attacked already, isn't that an indication that they intend using it as I've suggested?'

'I think that would be a dangerous deduction.'

The Lord President said, 'They must not find out that *we* know the submarine has foundered.' He glanced quickly at the First Sea Lord. 'Has the Captain been told to destroy our signals to him – the signals we have sent since the disaster?'

'No.'

The Lord President made a gesture of great impatience. 'He must be told to at once. Good God! It would be fatal evidence to fall into the Russians' hands! It would destroy our last hope.'

'Then if he's got to convince the Russians, he'll have to disable his radio receiver,' the First Sea Lord said. 'I cannot order him to do that.'

The Lord President's face was quivering with anger. 'First Sea Lord, there is a logic in this situation and I am not one to flinch from it!'

There was a bristling silence. Nobody seemed willing to break it. The Prime Minister shifted in his chair. 'I come back to the point that if the submarine has been disabled by the Russians' underwater defences or mines, they doubtless know already.'

'In other words, how is the Russian silence to be interpreted?'

The Prime Minister's eyes interrogated the Defence Chiefs.

The First Sea Lord shook his head. 'Impossible to say.' The others shook their heads too.

The Prime Minister said, 'I shall go to my study for ten minutes. Ministers will please stay in the building. I would like Montfalcon to return if he can.'

He got up and went out, followed by the Chief of the General Staff.

Outside the Cabinet Room, the Prime Minister turned left past Henning's and the secretaries' offices and climbed the stairs to the first floor. The Prime Ministers of the past watched from their frames lining the wall. He remembered their intimidating review when he had been the new arrival at Number 10. Now he rarely passed them by in the hard moments of political life without feeling their communion in his loneliness.

At the top he entered the small study and shut the door. The room was comfortably and elegantly furnished – settee, bookshelves, good pictures. His eyes went over the familiar objects – the desk which had belonged to Pitt, the photograph in the silver frame, the Fabergé box which had been a wedding present. In the redecoration some time back they had restored the light cream colouring to the walls, which the Prime Minister thought unimaginative. But the scrolled fireplace imported then was a successful touch. His mind sought momentary relief in these details.

He went to the window and stood looking out on to the dark garden below – the mass of the ilex and magnolia trees, the wall of Horseguards Parade and, beyond, the darkness of the Park. He stood for several minutes, scarcely moving. Everything was still. The tiny ticking of the clock was the only sound.

When he turned, he pressed a buzzer on his desk. Henning appeared and the Prime Minister asked for the Foreign Secretary to be sent up. A moment elapsed before the Foreign Secretary came. He looked a little pugnacious. Interviews in the Prime Minister's study were infrequent. The Prime Minister thought he must believe he had been called in for an explanation about allying himself with the Lord President.

The Prime Minister smiled gently. 'Come in. I think we must tell the Ambassador in Moscow. Have the telegram marked top secret, personal to the Ambassador. If he can find out whether the Russians know anything, so much the better.'

The Foreign Secretary pursed his lips. 'That would be too dangerous, I fear.'

'Convey to him, at all events, that any hint would be of the greatest value. It is extremely urgent.'

The Foreign Secretary nodded and went out. A moment later the door opened. Henning's head appeared with someone close behind, a short, dapper figure with trim white hair and a white moustache who pushed gently past him into the room. It was the Home Secretary.

'Arthur.' The Prime Minister turned with visible relief. He came forward with outstretched hand.

None other of the Ministers was on the same footing of intimacy with the Prime Minister. The two had known each other all their adult lives, longer even than the Prime Minister and the Lord President.

'You've been briefed?' the Prime Minister said as they shook hands. The Home Secretary nodded. They exchanged a look in which much was said.

'What shall we do?'

'I have a proposal,' the Home Secretary said. 'You must listen to it.'

'I will, Arthur.'

'You must make a public appeal to Kruschev,' the Home Secretary said. 'On the radio. Tell the BBC you want to make an emergency broadcast, go to the studio at once and have the thing translated into Russian and put out to them as you speak.

'You announce the submarine's plight, give the true position in Russian waters and say it's an accident. The submarine is not carrying missiles which proves she is not there with any aggressive design. But she must have help and you are appealing to Kruschev to step in. You give the number of survivors; say they are waiting for rescue. Kruschev can't refuse to save the men. Your message will be known all over the world in a

107

few minutes. He would condemn himself in the eyes of world opinion if he didn't respond.'

'That's what *we'd* think,' the Prime Minister said. 'He would see it quite otherwise. Anyway, it would mean our admitting that we had been in touch with the submarine beforehand. That would dreadfully detract from the force of the appeal, Arthur. We should obviously only be making the broadcast as a last resort because we couldn't do anything else, couldn't keep it hushed up.'

'Would it matter? It's surely the most dangerous thing to try to keep it quiet?'

The Prime Minister paced the room and came back. 'Kruschev, as you know, is in great difficulties. He would find it impossible to yield. He could pretend to accept – to disarm international opinion – and then say the Russian rescuers had arrived "too late". They would keep anybody else away from the area. Nobody would ever know what had happened. In any event, he would not accept the claim of an "accident". He couldn't afford to.'

'It is worth the gamble,' the Home Secretary said.

'But think of the effect on the country. Think of the shock – and the awful blow to the United States.'

The Home Secretary looked at him. There was agony in the Prime Minister's eyes.

CHAPTER NINE

THE WATERTIGHT DOOR between the compartment where Grimble and Beale were now together and the engine-room section which Punchard and the other five men shared, was a geared door. It was operated by turning a wheel on either side which slid it open or shut. At some moment after it had been shut by Punchard's group, this door had jammed, probably when the ship had hit the bottom. The jamming had naturally remained unnoticed until Grimble and Beale had made their presence known to Punchard's group on the other side and they all tried to join up by opening the door. Their combined efforts failed to move it. Because of his injury, Grimble was of hardly any help. But four of the six, all straining on the wheel on their side, and Beale at his, could not open it more than an inch. It looked as if cogs in the gearing were broken. But at least the men could speak to each other through the gap.

Hour after hour, Punchard and others by turns worked at the door. Sometimes they worked in conjunction with Beale, sometimes on their own. Sometimes they called to Beale, lying idle on the far side, to help with pressure on his wheel. At first he responded. But presently he began to pretend he didn't hear, then to take no notice. He seemed to resent Punchard's summonses and lay moody and lethargic for long periods. Grimble, who felt himself getting weaker, watched him. They did not speak much.

At times, Grimble woke from a painful doze and found Beale staring at the demolition control mechanism at one side of the compartment. This was a small steel case painted red with a glass panel and a handle fixed by a pin and a sealed wire. It looked something like the top of an ordinary fire alarm. The time delay was set on the visible dial and the handle pulled down; thereafter, when the time was reached, a tube of acid would break, start the mechanism to explode the charge. It was fitted with two safety devices. As soon as it was set, it started continuous alarm bells simultaneously in the compartment itself and in the control room. It could not be set for a shorter time than one hour ahead.

Beale seemed to be fascinated by the red demolition case. He lay watching it with a strange immobility. He began to go up to it and stand in front of it. Then he gripped the handle.

'What are you doing?' Grimble said. 'Got a fag, boy? (Beale had miraculously produced a full packet.) Let it alone.'

Beale turned round. He had an unnaturally wide grin.

'Shall I blow us all to Jesus?'

'Pipe down.'

'Better than this, wouldn't it?'

'Give a hand on the door, boy.'

'You couldn't stop me, Lofty, could you?'

There was a harsh metallic screech and a burst of voices. They both looked round. The door had suddenly given another two inches. Grimble noticed that Beale wasn't smiling any longer.

Leading ME Cubit was on his back on the mess table. Wingrove, glistening with sweat, was holding him down with Bosco. Cubit's mouth was open, his lips bloody. Blood from his nose had run down his face on to the table. There was an open cut on his cheek below one eye. Cubit was breathing heavily.

Petty Officer Fitch swung up to the table and made to throw a blow to his jaw.

'Lay off, for Christ's sake, Fitch!' Petty Officer Robertson caught Fitch's arm and wrenched him away. Fitch's face was distorted with anger, his lips drawn back from his teeth. He flung away, swearing. 'A bloody spy, a bloody saboteur.'

Cubit was grunting and gaspingly spitting blood and mucus. He moved his legs. 'Stay still, you bastard!' Bosco said. 'Or you'll get some more.' Haynes was seated on the nearer table watching Cubit's face. Savage and Green stood beside him, Green dabbing a cut lip. The mess benches were overturned and dominoes and other things scattered in the fight were strewn on the deck.

Fitch flung to the intercom. He was still out of breath with rage and exertion. He snatched the telephone and rang the Bridge. Nothing happened. Fitch viciously jabbed the buzzer again.

'Captain. Bridge,' the voice came back.

'Petty Officer Fitch, sir (his voice excited). We got the bloody bastard who sabotaged the ship with us here – Cubit. It's Cubit! We caught him with a detonator and he admits it! It was him who blew us up, he's proud of it, the tuckin' bleeder. He did it! He says so, a bloody Communist. He did it on purpose. What are we going to do with the bastard, sir . . .?'

'Fitch . . . Wait a minute . . . Wait —' Jason tried vainly to check the flow of words. '. . . Petty Officer Fitch!'

Abruptly Fitch stopped.

'What are you saying?' Jason said. 'What's happening there? Repeat it, slowly.'

Fitch got a grip on himself; he was still tense. 'We caught Leading ME Cubit with a detonator, sir. Bosco found him. He was hiding it under one of the tubes . . . What sir? . . . About half an hour ago, sir. Maybe a bit more. We didn't know what it was at first. He tried to make out it was nothing, then PO Robertson said it looked like a detonator. He tried to laugh it off. But we got hold of him. Then he said it was one, it was a detonator – and after Wingrove got hold of him, he says, "Well, you bastards, all of you, if you want to know who did the ship, I did. And I'd do it again, see?"'

'Haynes said he was just putting it on, but he said he wasn't. He'd been waiting for the chance, he said, to put the ship out of commission. . . . Sabotage, sir . . . What, sir? . . . Yes. Two, sir. He said he'd hid two explosive charges, the ones that went off, but he won't say where. Yes, sir, he come aboard with it. He'd got another detonator hid under the grease-gun by the lower port tube. We started laying into him and he answered back with a lot of Communist talk. He's a bloody Communist, he says. And long live Soviet Russia and peace, he says, and all that bull. No, sir . . . nothing more . . . I don't know, sir.

He's shut up now and won't say anything. What are we going to do with him, sir? Yes, sir ... No, sir. ... About half an hour ...' Fitch stood there answering Jason's questions, repeating the explanation. At last it was over. 'Aye, aye, sir.' Fitch took the telephone from his ear, stood holding it for a moment, then hooked up.

'What'd he say?' It was Haynes.

'Wanted to know if anything more was going off; and we have to keep the bastard watched.'

'He ain't going far,' Bosco said.

Silently, Robertson took one of Wingrove's arms. 'Let him get up, Tiny.'

Wingrove moved back. Bosco looked doubtful then let go too. Cubit rolled to the edge of the table and dropped off. As his feet touched the deck, he shot upright and threw a punch at Bosco. It landed on the side of Bosco's head, knocked him back and he tripped backwards over a bench.

Wingrove's massive arm was raised to smash Cubit but Robertson shouldered between them. 'Hold off, Tiny! You'll kill the bleeder.' He gave Cubit a shove in the chest, sending him back against the bulkhead. Cubit faced him, glowering, chin down, fists ready, spitting out bloody mucus.

'Sit down there, you. On the deck. Don't come anything funny or by Christ you'll get your lot I swear it.' Robertson's face was bone-pale; he seemed hardly able to get the words out.

'You creepin'-murderer!' Bosco, crouching, was going for him again, but Wingrove this time held him back.

'Go and —' Cubit spat. He stood glowering defensively for a minute. Then he sat on the deck. He pulled out a dirty handkerchief and began wiping his mouth and dabbing the cut on his face. He kept his eyes on the others.

'Leave the bastard.' They drew back, leaving the corner where he sat empty, separating themselves from him. Haynes remained seated on the table, simply shifting along it. He was a little closer to Cubit than the rest.

For a few minutes they continued to bawl obscenities and swear at Cubit. Then, in reaction, a quieter mood gradually

112

overcame them. Cubit sat dabbing at his swollen lips. From time to time he felt his eye which was now puffed, almost shut.

Fitch broke the long quiet spell. 'Well, the cow-son's come home to Russia, all right.'

'That's what I've been wondering about,' Haynes said quietly. Haynes had hardly spoken. He had sat quietly watching and since the fight it had seemed as if the balance between the men had shifted once again and Robertson's authority had taken over. But now, as Haynes spoke, the others looked at him as before. 'How did he know we were coming here, into Russian waters?'

Cubit was eyeing him with a mixture of contempt and defiance.

'I mean, is Mr Bloody Cubit a bigger fish than we think?' Haynes said.

'Yuh. How did he know otherwise?'

'That's right. How'd he know?'

Cubit said, 'I didn't. I didn't know any more than you did. It didn't make any difference to me. We might have been in the bloody Atlantic, it would have been all the same.'

'Yah!'

'Liar.'

'Orders from Moscow.'

Cubit shrugged. 'Believe what you like. Christ, I'm glad this is where we end up!'

'It's where you'll end up,' Wingrove said. 'Take it from me.'

Haynes was eyeing Cubit narrowly. 'Do you mean to say, you just —'

'Aw, go and —' Cubit made an obscene gesture. 'You think you know everything, don't you? Mr Bloody Sea Lawyer.' Suddenly he shouted, 'I been waiting months – months! And I got the better of them and their — security, didn't I?'

'How was it that you did it just on this trip, then?' Robertson said.

'It might have been last trip, next trip – any trip! And you don't like orders from Moscow, oh no! You want your orders from Washington and the imperialist camp, that's what you want. Sure I've had orders from Moscow and I'm proud of it. We had to strike a blow against the revanchard and aggressive imperialist designs and what's better than wrecking a nuclear submarine? Nobody could know it was going to be done here. But now it has been, the imperialist camp has suffered a smashing defeat.'

'What's this camp talk?' Wingrove said.

'Well, you won't be able to report to your Russian masters,' Robertson said.

Quietly Haynes said, 'Tell us, Cubit, what'd you do? Where'd you put the stuff? Must have been bloody powerful explosive.'

Cubit swore and mumbled in a low voice, averting his face.

'What was it, Cubit?'

'Go to hell.'

Savage stepped up to Haynes, stammering, 'But he's got to tell us! We could all get out of this, get the ship up if he says what he did!'

'Take it easy.'

Fitch said, 'What are we going to do with him, Dave? Torture him?'

'Make him talk.'

'Yes, go on.'

Fitch went to the intercom and rang it. Jason answered. Fitch said, 'What are we going to do with this bloody Commie? We got to make him talk, sir. If we know what he did maybe we can do something with the ship.'

Jason said, 'I don't think there's —'

'But we've got to make him say! He's been waiting months, he says, to do us. We've got to do him. He's going out in small pieces!'

'Petty Officer Fitch! Listen to me. You're the senior man in that section and you're expected to keep order. They want to beat him up, that's easy to understand. But it's up to you to keep them in check, good God man, not lead them on. Is that clear? *Is that clear?* Everybody would like to have a go at him. I don't doubt that. He'll get his deserts when we're out.

But till we are there's to be no nonsense and no violence. D'you hear? ... Fitch? ... D'you hear ...?'

'Aye, aye, sir.' Fitch rang off. The phone immediately buzzed again. Fitch ignored it.

Haynes swivelled on the table and said sarcastically, 'Is that clear, Fitch? When's he coming along here to stop us?'

'Let's kill the bastard.'

Vehemently, Cubit said, 'Do you think that's going to do you any good?' He shouted again, 'I ain't scared – and I can prove it because I didn't reckon to get out of this alive anyway.'

'A bloody Commie hero,' Robertson said, with disgust. 'Casabianca from Moscow.'

'Killed a lot of decent fellers,' Wingrove said.

'I'm one up on you lot. I got nothing to lose,' Cubit said. 'You're all scared to hell and I did my job.'

'Shut your mouth,' Wingrove said. 'Or I'll shut it for you.'

They turned away from him. But his words seemed to have made an impression. Cubit could have had small hope of escape after sabotaging the ship.

Fitch went into the torpedo compartment. Wingrove followed. Bosco slumped at the second table, chin in hand. Haynes sat cleaning his fingernails with a match. After a while, he got down and began walking slowly up and down between two of the tables.

Idly and aimlessly the seven men moved back and forth between the two compartments, exchanging a few words now and then, squatting down, rising again, leaning against a piece of machinery, twisting a handle, moving a lever, occasionally glancing at the clock, restless and uneasy, and all the time unconsciously listening for the beat of the scrubber.

It was perceptibly hotter in the mess. None of them knew the reason for this but they all felt it. Most of them had stripped down to singlets and dungarees. Wingrove was still naked except for his pants. Cubit nursed his cuts. Nobody stopped him when he went to the tap and bathed his bruised eye. He seemed to have regained confidence.

Haynes was the least restless of the men. He sat watching

Cubit. Cubit stared back. He held Haynes's eyes. Something was exchanged between them.

Cubit said, 'You said yourself it was spying, didn't you? What right have you got to come spying here? You haven't got any right. It's an international crime. It's contrary to international law and everybody on this ship's guilty.'

'All except you, I suppose?' Robertson said tensely.

'The power of Marxism and Leninism is going to defeat the imperialists' rotten designs, Robertson, and you may as well know it.'

'Dry up that Commie lingo.'

'Dry up! Dry up! If we'd come here to fire off missiles at Russia, you wouldn't even have known it. Would you? You'd have started a world war and you wouldn't know it! Who's finger on the trigger? Eh? No, it ain't the captain's. It's yours, yours and yours! So you're just cogs, are you? What do you care? Nothing! Would you protest – you? Not bloody likely. "Is that clear, Fitch? Aye, aye, sir!" Fry 'em all! Look lively there! A million Russians! Three million! Five million! Women and kids. "Aye, aye, sir." No more Moscow, Leningrad, Minsk, Kiev – whoof, whoof, whoof – finished, fried, up in smoke! That's what you're after, you and your masters. But you won't get away with it.'

'Shall we kill the bastard?' Wingrove said.

'You heard what the Old Man said.'

'Shut up, Fitch.' It was Haynes.

The others looked at Haynes. He hoisted himself up on the table again, took a cigarette butt from behind his ear and lit it. He blew out the smoke, looking round at them.

'We're in charge here. We'll decide what we're going to do. And what we're *not* going to do.'

Robertson turned his back and went into the torpedo compartment. The others said nothing.

Cubit made the rag into a pad, wet it and applied it to his eye. He held it there, looking over his shoulder at the mess. Only one light was burning.

Green, Savage and Bosco were stretched out asleep on the

deck. Petty Officer Fitch and Haynes were sprawled drowsily at the far table. The other two were sleeping in the torpedo compartment.

Cubit wet the pad and applied it again. He took a drink. He stood patting his eye gently with the wet rag. Presently he straightened up. He reached up to a shirt on a hook and took a packet of cigarettes from the pocket. Gingerly, wetting the end, he put one between his lips. He drew on it deep and turned round. Fitch and Haynes, leaning on the table, were watching him silently.

Cubit took another pull at the cigarette. He went towards them. He stepped over Bosco and sat down on the bench opposite. They all sat looking at each other. Cubit's expression was relaxed but alert. Haynes regarded him impassively. Fitch looked dumbly resentful.

'Smoke?' Cubit's voice was quiet. He held out the packet of cigarettes.

Haynes paused; then he reached out and took one. He broke it in two and passed half to Fitch without taking his eyes off Cubit.

Fitch took it and struck a match. Each of them applied the cigarette to the flame.

Cubit leant an arm on the table. They each took a draw or two.

'You're intelligent, Haynes, ain't you?' Cubit said.

Haynes grinned faintly. There was a pause.

'Know something?' Cubit said.

'I don't know anything.'

'You kill me and you'll be saying goodbye to your chances of getting out of this.'

Another pause. 'See that?' Cubit said.

'Maybe,' Haynes said. 'Fitch sees it, don't you, Fitch?'

Fitch looked at Haynes uneasily. 'What you talking about?'

Cubit said, 'What do you think's going to happen when we get picked up, Fitch?'

Sullenly Fitch shrugged.

Cubit said, 'There won't be a welcome committee waiting down on the beach. If you're lucky they'll take you for spies,

117

and the Russians give spies the real treatment. If they find out this was going to be an attack, they're going to shoot you, Fitch.'

Fitch said nothing.

'See?'

Fitch didn't answer.

'You won't get away with it by saying you didn't know. They won't believe you.'

Fitch said, 'Who's going to prove it?'

Cubit laughed – then winced, putting his hand to his mouth.

'You're forgetting Cubit,' Haynes said.

Cubit looked at Haynes and grinned. Then he looked back at Fitch. 'The only one the Russians are going to believe is me, Fitch. You'd better keep me in good health because I'm the only one who can give you a good character. I'm the only one who'll be able to tell them you didn't know where you were coming on this trip or what it was all about.'

'Is that clear, Fitch?' Haynes said. He grinned sarcastically.

'Maybe I could even get you off, Fitch – all of you,' Cubit said. 'Anyway, with a stretch in the clink. I'm your passport to safety.'

Behind them, Bosco stirred and got to his feet. He sat at the table eyeing Cubit.

'Hear that, Bosco?' Haynes said.

Bosco nodded. 'I heard.'

'Bosco knows what's what, don't you, Bosco?' Cubit said, grinning again.

Bosco eyed him uncomfortably.

'Smoke?' Haynes said. Bosco's glance went to the packet of cigarettes on the table. Cubit shoved it towards him. Bosco hesitated, then took one, lit it.

The scene was being enacted slowly and deliberately as if each of them sensed, without formulating it to himself, that a great deal would turn on it. Cubit's footing with the others was changing.

'You know the Russians are soon going to spot us,' Cubit said.

'Why should they?' Fitch said, still sullen.

'Look, Fitch, we're in territorial waters. That means ten miles from the coast.'

'Or under,' Haynes said.

'Sure. Or under. And we're in two hundred and seventy feet of water.'

'Christ Almighty,' Fitch said.

'If you ask me, the chances are they know we're here already,' Cubit said.

Bosco and Fitch exchanged a quick glance.

'Don't you reckon so, Haynes?' Cubit said.

Haynes nodded. 'Fair chance they do.'

'Then why ain't they done anything about it?' Fitch said.

Cubit considered him with condescension. He was much more sure of himself now. 'They got their reasons. They're having a little game with us. Maybe they're going to bring us up and put us all on show. Caught in the bloody act, eh? How d'you like to be in the spotlight, Fitch? Remember Gary Powers, the U2 pilot? They put him on show all right, didn't they? Caught in the bloody act. His wife divorced him afterwards, remember?'

'How many kids you got, Fitch?' Haynes said.

'I didn't make out the orders,' Fitch said.

'Now you're startin' to see sense, Ginge,' Cubit said.

'Just a lot of guinea-pigs,' Haynes said. Their eyes went quickly to him. Deliberately, Haynes said again, 'That's all we are – just a lot of bloody guinea-pigs.' Bosco nodded.

Fitch swung away on his seat, then turned back. 'How do we know he ain't tellin' a pack of lies' (indicating Cubit). 'He's always blowing his trumpet, about what he's done and what he knows and don't you understand this and don't you understand that and don't you see what's behind the other. Look at the line he shot about those two tarts in Greenock and about getting 'em into the hotel and all that. Bull, that's all it was.'

'That was different, Fitch.' They shook their heads. They were not convinced.

'Listen, Ginge,' Cubit said, convincing them easily now. 'If we hadn't have come unstuck here, you'd never have known we'd all been sold down the river as spies – maybe worse –

would you? Well, would you?'

Fitch said nothing.

'Who told you they were going to make an international criminal out of you? Nobody? All right, you say you didn't know. The Old Man comes up with that bloody line about "if you're caught, you say you're not responsible". That's all bull. The Germans said that after the war, the war criminals. They were only acting under orders, they said – the generals, the field-marshals even, right down to the common soldiers and sailors, were only acting under orders of the Nazis and most of the Nazis were under Hitler's orders. But at that rate nobody's to blame for anything. You can't commit international crimes, crimes against humanity, do what you like and then hide behind orders. It's no excuse. You can't get away with that.'

'We were hoodwinked into coming here,' Fitch said vehemently. 'We ought to have been told. If they want to send people on trips like this, let 'em call for bloody volunteers. Sending married men with families . . . Christ!'

Cubit leaned eagerly forward, fist raised to jab home some further argument. Suddenly he stopped. They all froze. An irregular knocking was coming from outside. It approached fairly quickly along the hull, a series of knocks, taps and bumps, and passed aft.

Fitch wet his lips.

'That's the second time,' Haynes said.

'Was that a bloody frogman?' Bosco said.

'Hold it!'

Nobody moved. They sat tensely listening.

CHAPTER TEN

JASON HEARD THE sound on the bridge. He was sleeping with the shallowness acquired by master mariners which enables them to rest but wake instantly at something unusual. He sat up on the chart table. In the darkness he strained to identify the sounds as they passed aft. He stared out of the bridge porthole. There was no light.

Connor moved in the compartment above where he slept. He called down, 'Clyde – do we knock back?'

'No!'

The sounds stopped. Jason switched on the light as Connor came down the ladder. 'What was it?' Connor said.

'Don't know. I've heard it before. Could be a plate broken loose or something drifting.'

'Or tapping for us?'

'Didn't sound like it somehow.'

'Do you think it means they've come across us?'

'We'd hear more if they had, I think; and they'd show a light. I couldn't see a thing.'

'Unless they think we're still seaworthy and we're lying here for some purpose.'

'Don't you think they'd kill us if they thought that? Maybe not.'

'Perhaps they're out to fish us up alive and put us on international exhibition, like Powers and Wynne and so forth.'

'They wouldn't mind the chance.'

Jason swung his legs off the chart table and stretched. He made an entry in the log, looked up at Connor. 'Were you sleeping?'

Connor shook his head. 'Mind if I sit down?'

Jason gestured assent.

'What I cannot understand is why we haven't any emergency orders,' Connor said. 'I've been racking my brains for a reason and I can't find one. Why in God's name couldn't they see this possibility?'

'It was a mistake, an oversight.'

'But good God, it's inconceivable! They are all sailors, all professionals, all men of great experience, not a crowd of dockside civvies or politicians. They must have gone over and over the details, weighed the pros and cons and the risks and the chances. And yet here we are, simply left and told to keep quiet. I don't understand how it can happen.'

Jason looked at him with commiseration. He saw the pain of Connor's baffled perplexity. 'But what the hell, life is full of it – not the gods, just human fallibility. You get all the power of manifold intelligence brought to bear on something, some problem – as I'm sure it was on this mission – and some aspect escapes it, the blunder's made. It's an illusion to believe that men control events. Nobody in history ever controlled events for more than a tiny space of time. There's something mysterious about the way events take over. Men as blind victims, or damn nearly, for all but very little of the time and "events" mysteriously generated somewhere beyond, the complexity of other men's wills engendered in a million places at once pushing against you. All the cleverest men can do is to try to give a certain direction to things.

'Look at the mistakes that have been made by the best minds, the professionals, at judging people and motives and handling public affairs, first-class men. Look at the First World War when the best politicians and military men and diplomats went ludicrously wrong! After the Russian revolution, for instance, the Allies came to the conclusion that the Germans were going to attack Russia through Finland. They thought the Germans were going to attack the Murmansk–Petersburg railway. It was a complete mistake. *Now* we know, but they were facing a tremendously complex situation then and they didn't know the Germans were sending men into Finland simply to help the White Guard get Finnish independence. But the sharpest brains among the Allies, inside Russia and outside, were sure they were going to the railway. So we put men ashore in Murmansk and that was the beginning of intervention. Awful mistake! Yet the big men had poured over the facts, deliberated on them for months, had access to extensive information. Things get too difficult for men to see where they're going.

'We were told that the Russians were arming a million and a half German, Austrian and Rumanian prisoners in Siberia who were going to be used against the Allies. This was rubbish – complete rubbish! Yet the best minds accepted it. Balfour was urging Wilson, the American President, to approve of Japanese intervention in Russia because, so said Balfour, the Germans had crushed the Russian army and would never allow it to be built up again. This was conveyed to Wilson by Balfour on the very day that Trotsky was announcing the creation of the Red Army! Balfour and Wilson were clever men, full of experience. Their mistakes were ludicrous! If you try to trace it back you get single individual mistakes which you have to admit are simply mistakes. And that is the stuff of history.

'I once heard a very clever friend of my father's give a description of Asquith at a dinner. The whole company was a gathering of brilliant men, men of the finest intelligence and achievements. But as they sat there, it was plain that Asquith was more dazzling than even the best of them. Even among them, he was unmistakably the top man. Yet a few weeks later events simply brushed Asquith aside. He was inadequate. Perhaps controlling events is simply, for a little while, not making mistakes – like this.'

Connor said, 'Somebody has to pay for the inadequacy – and this time it's us. Who wants to go out through a mistake? I mean, knowing it's a mistake only makes you feel more damned helpless and frustrated. Doesn't it?'

'Sure.' They were silent for a few moments.

Jason said, 'You get some comfort from religion, don't you? You used to, at any rate.'

'Oh, used to. Not any more.' Connor's tone was impatient. He paused. Abruptly his face was congested. 'I believed in the bloody Navy! That was my religion, because it was decent and not like the stinkers in politics and the business jungle where you grovel and kiss the boss's arse every day. And it's

123

failed. It's turned out with this fumbling bloody failure! They didn't see this coming, perhaps they didn't care, and they've put paid to half the men, this ship is going to be blown to hell by a lot of Russians and for nothing. For a bit of stupidity! Let's put it over the bloody intercom!' He stopped himself and turned away. Presently he turned round. 'Sorry, Clyde.'

'It's all right.'

'Went off the rails. Bloody silly. No reason.'

'Sure.'

Jason held out his cigarettes. Connor looked at the packet, then questioningly up at Jason. Jason said, 'Won't make much difference.'

They lit the cigarettes. The match burned yellow in the dim light. Jason put the match in the ashtray.

'How long have we got?' Connor said.

'I dunno. Two days – three days? If that scrubber holds.'

'Seems a bit erratic. Must have taken a knock.'

The smoked in silence. The cigarettes, after their abstinence, tasted good. Connor leant on the chart table. The chart of the area lay open on it. Connor leant over, only moving to put the cigarette to his lips and draw, staring at the chart as if there were some explanation to be read there. He sighed deeply and looked up.

'What do you think they're doing?'

Jason didn't answer. Then he said, 'God knows.'

'Anything?'

'Not easy. I did send that signal asking for assistance.'

Connor was leaning against the chart table. He looked at the smoke from the cigarette rising in a barely wavering line. He reached out and stubbed it in the ashtray. They both watched the movement, hearing the crisp, pleasant sound of the ash against the metal. Jason still had a little of his to smoke.

'What do you believe in?' Connor said. He wasn't looking at Jason. Jason took a last draw on his cigarette, then reached and crushed it out.

'I mean, d'you believe in God?' Connor said.

'No. Sometimes I'd like to try but I don't. Religion's dead and what are you going to put in its place? Socialism? Oh, you could once. You could be an Englishman or a Russian and a good man and believe that you were going to create a better world with socialism. They used to sing Blake's words about building a new Jerusalem in England's green and pleasant land. You could die for it, as thousands did, spend your life in the struggle for it. You've got to have something to die for. All right, socialism has come; and as an inspiration it's dead – a corpse! Socialism is just a political party label. There were people who could die for nationalization. Christ, the utopia that nationalization was going to usher in! And who believes in that any more?

'There aren't any more impulses for men. No more high and noble ones, anyway. Revolution used to be one. You used to be able to live for the great and noble ideas of *the* Revolution, any revolution, with a capital R. Liberty – marvellous and inspiring as long as the struggle lasts. But the revolutions are all succeeding. So liberty arrives and the high and noble impulse runs away into the sand – and you're left with a feeling of despair and emptiness.

'Do you know, the old revolutionaries would tell you that the people to be envied now are the American Negroes, the blacks of South Africa, the Spanish workmen, the milling millions of Asia, the people who still have the exaltation of struggle to live for, to give them a god to die for! Christ, it sounds barbaric, but maybe they're the last fortunate people on earth! Then, one day, they're going to get what they've fought for and they'll find their souls as empty as ours are. Perhaps that's when the bombs will bring civilization to an end and the process will begin all over again. In the meantime it's their bellies not their souls that are empty and they have their work cut out getting enough to eat – but nobody ever found that uplifting.

'The days of Auguste Comte, Proudhon, Fourier – wonderful men – when you could believe that men were perfectible and society could be brought to grace and harmony by institutions, they've gone for ever. The age of reason has gone the same way as the age of faith – *and it isn't progress*.

'What are you going to believe in today? Television? Stocks

125

and shares? Abstract painting? Look at it, look where we've come! We've reached the end. When I see pictures in the papers of religious hysteria in Italy, the intense religiosity in Spain and Ireland, all right it's bigotry, but by God, isn't it better than the telly? There aren't even any film stars to believe in any more! People used to believe in Mary Pickford and Lilian Gish – really be inspired by them. Girls used to see their pictures and say, well, they're poor and have a rough time too, like us, and we love 'em for it and believe in 'em. Oh, what the hell.' He broke off. 'Gone too far now to improve.'

Steps came up the ladder from below. It was Kirby. He saluted. 'Just taken the news bulletin, sir. Thought you'd like to see it.'

'Thanks, Kirby.' Jason took the sheets. 'Everything all right?'

'Aye, sir.'

'Good. Good night.'

'Good night, sir.' Kirby went down.

Jason put the sheets, written out in Kirby's simple clear hand, on the chart table. They bent over them reading. They turned the first sheet, read to the end of the second, but there was no mention of *Uranus* or any rescue operations.

'Shall we post it up?' Connor said.

'Why not? Let's face it,' Jason said crisply.

CHAPTER ELEVEN

THE PRIME MINISTER opened the door of the Cabinet Room and went in. The lights were still burning. There was the smell of tobacco smoke. The Prime Minister halted just inside, his eyes on the windows. The curtains had paled and a raw strip of daylight showed. Morning already. All night he had been terribly aware of the passing minutes, yet now the hours seemed to have crept up on him.

The Prime Minister shut the door behind him. He was alone. He crossed to the window and pulled the curtains back. The light was cold, blue and harsh. It looked as if it were going to be a grey and rainy day. He passed his hand over his face, squeezing the inner corners of his eyes. He had not slept but he felt reasonably fresh. He stood looking out of the window.

How much longer could it be before the country knew? The secret emergency evacuations would soon have to start, the dispersal centres quietly be brought to readiness to avoid public panic, the regional dictators who would rule the different areas of England under nuclear attack as delegates of government – since central government would no longer be possible – would have to be sent to their posts. The hundreds of radio posts by which proclamations, instructions, news, orders, notices of every kind would be broadcast to the population deprived of all other communication would have to be manned. The food depots, the emergency water and medical supplies which would have to tide them over when the ports were blocked and all the economic life, all ordinary activity, came to a standstill, would have to be guarded.

The Prime Minister shuddered. He felt a terrible sense of insufficiency. Naturally they had looked to civil defence. A great deal had been done in the past years, a proof of which was the organization which would soon go into action. Yet it was terrifyingly little. How could they have borne the burden of yet more cost on top of the immense defence budgets to provide all that they knew was necessary for civil defence? How could they have imposed yet more crushing taxation? Of course they couldn't – and they had gambled. They had gambled like all their allies, except the Americans who could afford not to; and even the Americans were far short of what was needed in civil defence. The Russians, he was confident, had nothing beyond the barest necessities for keeping a form of government in being while the attack was pressed.

There had been a period, in the early fifties, when civil defence was being mapped out in appalled secrecy, when officials in a special NATO department, with an Englishman at its head, had coldly tabulated the millions of dead to be expected and laboured at an infinity of detail necessary for keeping something going in the ash-strewn rubble of England. At one time the Lord President had been in charge of civil defence.

But then the effort had gradually been allowed to run down. Arguments had been found for believing that less and less was necessary. It was no good frightening people, they were told: do more harm than good. Besides, tension was easing; the Russians had other worries on their hands. And they had listened only too willingly.

There had been many moments when the incongruity between the insistence on an independent deterrent and the great gaps in protection had forced itself upon them. But they had preferred to turn away from it. They had preferred to believe that the deterrent would deter. For there was another incongruity they had not wanted to face either. They had proclaimed that the threat of a thermonuclear holocaust would be too terrible for any country to start one, and they had relied on this, permanently, to meet all circumstances. Yet if you believed it, then there could be no threat on your part. Somebody would take you at your word one day – and strike.

A bird alighted in the ilex tree in the garden. The Prime Minister watched it. It stayed for a moment then flew off.

There were also, the Prime Minister knew only too well, fearful inadequacies in the country's defences. The V-bombers could not be sent up in readiness to strike at Russia because of their short endurance. They must be kept on the ground until the warning system announced an attack on its way. It had been planned that when strained relations developed with Russia, the V-bombers would disperse in small groups so as to be less vulnerable. They had planned in terms of strained relations! The Prime Minister groaned inwardly. But at least the bombers had now been scattered.

On the other hand, the dispersal reduced the rapidity of their strike and complicated the task of refuelling them from the limited tanker force. Though there was none of the rush transport system as in America, no cars permanently turning over to speed crews out to the planes, the air chiefs claimed that they could get the aircraft off the ground in four minutes. He doubted this – and what might not happen in that thirty-second margin before the megatons began falling on Britain? Even so, could the bombers get through the tremendous defence zone which the Russians had built up in East Germany and Poland, far ahead of Russian territory?

The Prime Minister lit a cigarette. There were the TSR2s which were to have had a leading place in Britain's independent striking force. They had talked of putting one hundred and fifty TSR2s into service. But it had proved impossible to build anything like that number. The costs were staggering. The TSR2s had turned out to cost £4 million apiece.

Enormous sums again had been spent on the Bloodhounds – with what result? With anguish, the Prime Minister thought of it. The Bloodhound, they had believed, would provide superb anti-aircraft defence for the British Isles. But when they had developed Mark I they found the aircraft it was intended to destroy had doubled their speed. They had developed Mark II, a splendid weapon. But by this time the cost had forced them to recognize that they could only use Bloodhounds to defend the V-bomber bases in East Anglia. Set in their concrete sites, the Bloodhounds were certainly targeted by the Russians. But under the dispersal system, the V-bombers would no longer, in an alert, be at the bases. The Bloodhounds, moreover, were meant to hit aircraft and would be powerless against the missiles with which the Russians could wipe out sites and bases simultaneously.

His mind turned to the Fleet. The plan had been to sail vast convoys once a month, the ships two and three miles apart, protected by escorts and submarines. But on its own, the Navy had nothing like the escorts needed, scarcely two dozen in home waters. This was not so black as it looked, they had thought, since in a crisis there would be the Dutch with them, the Americans, the Norwegians, the Germans, the French, the whole of NATO.

At every turn of defence, they had assumed that others would be with them. The defence planners, the specialists, above all the Americans, had considered the alternative preposterous. The Prime Minister remembered a day when he had asked the Defence Planning Staff about the contingency plan for independent British defence and attack – and their looks as they told him how they had dug the plan out from the bottom of the contingency list and 'dusted it off'.

The Prime Minister felt bitter distress. It had simply not been possible to do everything. The British people had deserved a little prosperity after so many hard years.

The Prime Minister turned from the window. Deliberately he cast thoughts of these things from his mind. Now he must confront something else. Nearly an hour before, he had taken a hard decision. He must, he felt, inform the Leader of the Opposition of the crisis. He had been sent for and would be here in a short time.

The decision had been hard, since the Prime Minister sincerely believed the Leader of the Opposition to be a dangerous man.

Oliver Messender had had an unimpaired, even brilliant, career in his party. The only manifest hitch in his life had occurred before he had entered politics. He had intended going into international finance, nursed it as an ambition since adolescence and been encouraged in it by his family (whom the Prime Minister knew as rich and *arriviste*). He had triumphed

130

at school and the university and successfully passed a competitive examination for an executive post in the International Bank. He was the foremost of three remaining candidates. Then, at this very final stage, a senior member of the Bank had met him at a dinner party. Messender had been eliminated. His family managed to get an appeal made. He was asked to a country-house weekend with the other candidates – and was failed again, finally and irrevocably.

The Prime Minister had always regarded this as one of the most brilliant pieces of psychological insight he had ever come across. He had himself discovered the weaknesses in Oliver Messender's character only by much longer and closer observation – and not all those in the Opposition ranks were yet alive to them.

Messender was a clever dissimulator. After his failure with the International Bank – which could not have blocked a career in finance elsewhere – he had turned impetuously to politics. The Prime Minister would not allow himself to question the conviction with which he held his party's doctrines. He had joined the party under the aegis of a venerated member of the old guard who had died six months later. The new leaders of the party, keen to show their emancipation, had given him rough treatment. He had accepted repeated humiliation from them. He had crawled. He had toadied. He had tried to flatter them by inviting them to his house and displaying his rich friends and his family's rich friends.

Slowly he had ingratiated himself. Whenever he spoke out an opinion and was opposed from above, he never made more than a symbolic fight, never protested, but yielded and assumed his leaders' views even to his close associates.

He was given a post in the shadow cabinet, then another. He rose. At country-house weekends he entertained men he despised and even loathed but who were powerful or had the ear of the leaders. The Prime Minister had heard him called 'smarmy', but that was far too simple a conception. It was the innate sense of intrigue in him, a deviousness, a snakiness that called up profound mistrust.

When the Opposition party leader had been killed in an air

crash, there had been a brief, savage struggle at the top and Messender had taken over.

He was all that was amiable and agreeable outwardly – short but well-made with a dark-complexioned face and dark curling hair, large luminous eyes, a fine horseman and tennis-player. He had a slow, intense manner. But in the course of their political contests and their many inevitable associations, the Prime Minister had also discovered utter ruthlessness in him. For a time the Prime Minister had believed it sprang from his uncertainty in the leadership, a sense of insecurity. But he had been obliged to recognize that it was something else.

Ruthlessness, the Prime Minister knew, is a quality which ordinary men cannot deal with. Men working together accept certain characteristics, they arrive tacitly at a set of conditions and rules of behaviour. But ruthlessness is outside all these. It makes ordinary men as a group extremely uncomfortable, disintegrates them. They cannot cope with it. And Messender, the Prime Minister observed, was ruthless to an intense degree.

It was the rarest thing, the Prime Minister knew, to find impetuousness in a character of this sort. Yet, apart from the evidence of the change of career, it had come to his ears that Messender had a blazing, some said pathological, temper which at times prostrated him with headaches and at others caused him to humiliate party subordinates. The Prime Minister thought he was not an entirely upright man and shrank at the notion of him as head of Her Majesty's government.

The telephone on the Prime Minister's desk buzzed softly. The Prime Minister turned and lifted the receiver. Henning's voice said, 'Mr Messender is here, Prime Minister.'

'Show him in.' The Prime Minister looked at his watch. It was ten minutes to five. As the door opened, he went to the end of the long table and greeted the Leader of the Opposition.

Messender was smiling cautiously; but his eyes were narrowed. He entered briskly, as if to give the impression that he was quite used to being alert at this hour, though his collar and tie proclaimed hasty dressing. His eyes were going quickly round the room for clues to the summons.

'Good morning,' the Prime Minister said. 'I'm sorry to get you out of bed so early.'

'Oh – fresh morning drive,' the Leader of the Opposition said, the smile extending a little. 'One sees London at its best at this hour.'

At the Prime Minister's gesture he sat at the table beside the central armchair. The Prime Minister took his usual place. Once, when the Prime Minister had called on him at the Opposition's private office in the House, the interview had proceeded with the Leader of the Opposition seated behind his desk and the Prime Minister in a very low chair on the other side. The Prime Minister had reflected with amusement that he must seem somewhat like an applicant for a job. That was typical of Messender.

Now he declined when the Prime Minister held out a box of cigarettes. Without preliminaries, the Prime Minister plunged in. 'A disaster has occurred to one of our submarines and we may be under Russian attack at any moment without knowing where it is going to take us. In these circumstances, it is my duty to give you the full facts.'

As the Prime Minister talked, the Leader of the Opposition's face darkened. He fidgeted a little with his hands. He took a cigarette case from his waistcoat pocket and lit a cigarette. He held it between the second and third fingers of his hand and when he had filled his mouth with the smoke, he seemed not to know what to do with it and let it out in gusts which he had to wave away. But his attention was sharp. Twice as the Prime Minister proceeded, he said 'Good God!' in a low voice and looked away. The Prime Minister waited, then resumed. The Leader of the Opposition asked a question or two; then, as the Prime Minister finished, he got up.

'My God, what a situation – this is frightful.' Nervously he stubbed out the cigarette, walked round the table, swung about. 'Is there a danger of radiation?'

'We think not.' The Prime Minister was also on his feet. At some stage earlier, at some immeasurable distance back it now

133

seemed, the Prime Minister had himself asked the same question. He reached back towards it now, beyond the comings and goings, the gatherings of anxious faces, the telephone calls and the too-numerous cigarettes. The First Sea Lord had summoned Rear-Admiral (Submarines), the naval experts and the Scientific Adviser and they had gone into it.

'I don't want to be reassured,' the Prime Minister said. 'I want facts. Could the submarine's reactor explode – like an atomic bomb?'

'No, sir,' Rear-Admiral (Submarines) said. 'It is impossible for the nuclear reactor to explode in that way. It is designed to minimize that sort of risk and it is protected against underwater corrosion. In a disaster of this sort, the fuel elements would remain intact.'

The Prime Minister's eyes went questioningly to the Scientific Adviser, who nodded. 'Let us suppose,' the Scientific Adviser said, 'that the reactor was working normally when the disaster happened. If they then had a leak for some reason in the fuel chamber – the part that contains the uranium – then the sea rushing in would cool the core of fuel and you wouldn't have any melting or explosion.'

The Prime Minister said, 'With the reactor completely submerged the radioactive materials would not be released?'

The Rear-Admiral said, 'It can remain submerged indefinitely without that happening, sir.'

'As it is,' the Scientific Adviser said, 'we dump radioactive material in the sea, in containers, of course. If you wanted to get rid of a nuclear reactor, probably one of the safest things to do with it would be to dump it at the bottom of the sea, in deep water.'

'But this is not deep water and it is very close to the Russian coast.'

'That is an unfavourable element,' the Scientific Adviser said.

'Is there any way in which these radioactive materials could be released?' the Prime Minister asked.

'The only way would be if the fuel rods were to melt and the shielding and the very strong pressure system we use to

134

enclose the reactor were to shatter.'

'Then they could escape? There would be a danger of radioactivity?'

The Read-Admiral said, 'There are five separate automatic devices, air, to prevent the fuel melting,'

'On the hypothesis that all these devices fail?' the Prime Minister said.

'Supposing the reactor were broken up,' the Scientific Adviser said, 'it couldn't, of course, go on producing the chain reaction. The fuel would be dispersed as pieces of metal and they would eventually corrode and gradually release radioactivity.'

'It would?'

'Yes. But that would be dispersed and diluted by the sea.'

'Nevertheless, given the depth and the proximity to land and, in the worst possible circumstances, of all the safety devices failing, you cannot say that there is absolutely no danger?'

'No. It cannot be absolutely ruled out. But it seems to me to be a very slight possibility. It would depend on what exactly has happened and how it has happened, which is what we do not know. But if those men are alive it tends to show that nothing so absolute as a complete break-up of the reactor and the melting of the rods has occurred.'

They had not been able to go beyond that.

Now, in the Prime Minister's office, Messender's look became more intense as the Prime Minister finished explaining this.

'But a slight possibility, heavens, the risk is there! You cannot let it subsist, man. It is the equivalent to an act of war. You must warn the Russians.'

The Prime Minister said coldly, 'I think I must decide that.'

The Leader of the Opposition turned away. The Prime Minister caught the expression of calculation. From the window, Messender said, 'Have you brought me here to tell me all this only when you decided I could not use the facts publicly against you?'

In spite of himself, the Prime Minister felt a stab of anger; but he controlled it. That also was so like Messender! He said, 'No, but because it is in the national interest. It is my duty.'

There was a pause. Both men were silent. Messender seemed absorbed by his thoughts. Then he said, 'Are you telling the Americans?'

'Not yet.'

Before Messender could interject, the telephone rang. The Prime Minister took it. 'Yes?' Henning was on the other end, saying that the Lord President had come back and wanted to see the Prime Minister. 'In a moment,' the Prime Minister said and rang off.

He turned back to the Leader of the Opposition. 'There is something else you must know. The submarine was fitted with certain items of American equipment. They were very sophisticated devices which the President let us have without formal Congressional authority, so that we might have our nuclear submarines operating now.

'When they were pushing us to bring the Polaris programme forward, we explained to the President that we could do so but that our development of these items was holding us up. The submarines would not, therefore, be up to the American submarines' performances and certain awkwardness in joint operations would result. The President thereupon agreed to let us have these items. By the same occasion, we pressed him for another one, a new sonar, and he let us have that as well. That is also in *Uranus*.'

The Leader of the Opposition made a low exclamation. 'Awful!' His eyes went to the Walpole portrait. In a moment he said, 'The Russians, of course, may *never* say they have captured the ship and have our secret material and the American gear.'

A typical Messender touch, the Prime Minister thought.

'That we cannot tell,' he said. 'But on personal grounds, I think Kruschev would have more to gain by exploiting the incident against us than by hushing it up. You know his difficulties.'

The Leader of the Opposition seemed not to have heard. Musingly he said, 'They could *deny* having located the submarine or raised it or found the secret gear. We could hardly prove it!'

The Prime Minister gave him a close look. This deviousness of mind sometimes terrified him.

'You can't keep silence,' Messender said.

'What do you propose?'

Messender rocked twice up and down on his toes. 'That is not my role, Prime Minister,' he said. 'You must admit your mistake.'

'I think it has gone beyond admitting mistakes. We are under the risk of imminent attack.'

'Broadcast! Tell Kruschev you've bungled!' The dark, intense look in Messender's face had become remarkably pronounced. The Prime Minister groaned inwardly. This was his crucifixion. It was what he wanted most to do, to admit the mistake, to confess it openly. But that was what, for higher motives, he felt he dared not do. And to have it come from Messender was almost beyond endurance.

He said, 'I ask you to reflect. How are we to tell them? They would believe we had told them only because we failed, because of this accident, this disaster, and that our true purpose in sending the submarine there had been a creep attack – on the Chizha installations if not farther afield. Or that at least it was a reconnaissance preparatory to attack. I hear your objection already: "Oh, but they would know that was not so, since we have no other attack mounted. We couldn't dare to attack Russia by surprise with one submarine."

'I have already told you that we have gone to the first degree of readiness. We felt we were bound to do this to defend ourselves if they come at us. *Now it is too late to say "We were not going to attack you".* Our planes are dispersed. Our fuelling tankers are in the air. The Fleet is at sea. We have recalled ships from the Baltic, and so forth. We know it was *defensive*. They would be entitled to think it *offensive*. At this moment, the Russians may be alerted to some of our air activity. Besides, if a surprise attack were ever to be made, it might be made in such conditions. Who can tell? There are no rules. It is unknown territory.

'There are no Polaris missiles on board the ship. Yet the Russians might genuinely be persuaded that the crew had had orders to jettison the missiles in the event of a mishap – as, indeed, they would. It would be impossible to persuade them otherwise.

'But in any event, it need make no difference to the Russians even if we did persuade them. It need make no difference if they were fully convinced that we had no intention of attacking them. Because this presents them with a unique opportunity.

'This *could* be the opportunity for a crushing blow at the western world. There are, I fear, very serious chances that, once they know the facts, the Americans will not threaten Russia with nuclear reprisals and risk their own complete national annihilation on account of this submarine. The Russians will immediately realize this – that the Americans will not come to our help in these circumstances.

'These therefore might well seem, to the Russians, the unique circumstances when the risk of an all-out thermonuclear attack on England would be worth their while. Think of it! They might well consider it worth the price of whatever damage we could do them, which would be comparatively small and would, alas, scarcely breach their nuclear potential, to reduce this country to wreck and rubble and leave them towering over western Europe, facing America alone. They may think it will have to happen some day and find these are suddenly better conditions than they had hoped for – a chance to eliminate England without war with America.

'It sounds hideous – monstrous. But we are not dealing with good House of Commons men.' The Prime Minister stopped speaking. The Leader of the Opposition had listened in silence. 'Would you,' the Prime Minister said, 'would you breathe a whisper, so long as there was the smallest hope of avoiding such a terrible outcome?'

The Leader of the Opposition was staring at the Prime Minister's place at the table. He seemed deeply abstracted. In

138

a moment he looked up. 'Have I your leave to inform my friends?'

'I cannot withhold you the right. I implore you to do so with the utmost discretion and to enjoin the strictest secrecy on them.'

The Leader of the Opposition moved towards the door.

'The government will be taking emergency powers by proclamation,' the Prime Minister said. 'I will keep you informed.'

The Leader of the Opposition nodded and went out.

The Prime Minister gave himself a moment before having the Lord President brought in. He sensed the portents of a critical interview. He felt suddenly very tired. He knew that with an hour's sleep he would awaken refreshed enough to continue throughout the day which stretched with awful infinity ahead. He lifted the telephone and spoke to Henning.

'Bring the Lord President in in ten minutes. Ring me on this telephone just before you come. Don't disturb me until then.' He replaced the receiver and went to the bookcase by the window and sank into the leather armchair there, the single chair for relaxation in the room. He shut his eyes. He had not the faculty of dropping off for a moment or two, the blessed gift which had helped famous men before him like Napoleon and Lloyd George through the worst periods. But even ten minutes' repose was precious.

All round him the house was quiet. Abruptly, as though some protective, healing mechanism had come into play, his mind turned away to the past, to the period he had spent in Paris as a young man.

He had lived far from the Sorbonne and far from his friends from Passy and the XVI arrondissement, in the Marais, the mysterious and haunted district on the north side of the rue Saint Antoine, full of decaying seventeenth- and eighteenth-century houses, façades with locksmiths' and toymakers' and tinsmiths' signs all over them and monumental staircases falling into ruin and the sudden surprises of fine courtyards. He had lived in three upper rooms in a house belonging to an old woman, a woman of a great family. The house, with its fore

139

courtyard walled to the street and its stone staircase and twenty-foot-high ceilings, was a magnificent ruin. But in it, the Prime Minister had felt the grand siècle and the French revolutionary past breathing with him and closely enclosing him.

In the evenings, when he had left some café in the Boul' Mich' or taken the Metro after seeing his friends, he had walked up the rue Payenne and regained the house with eagerness and an awed pleasure which never failed.

The old woman, Madame de Vizille, had been part of the pleasure. She was well over seventy, a woman of immense culture. She enchanted him in their talks which went on for hours in her gracefully dilapidated drawing-room. She had no family. They became great friends. She had grown old in a way quite pleasant to look at, she had the French wit and insight and sense of the past and a memory for stories about people which, while they amused him and often made him burst out laughing, threw sudden, dazzling shafts of illumination on events, on whole tracts of history, on motives and connections. And it was not only about France that she talked to him but many other countries. She had been a traveller in her youth.

When he was going to leave for home, she had said she would like to give him a little present. But it appeared that she had mislaid it. She would send it to him when she found it. A month later, back in London, he had received a package. It had been wrongly addressed and much delayed. He opened it and found a note from her, a month old, saying this was the gift she had been looking for. It was an album of colour-prints by Hokusai.

He was breathtaken. The colour-prints, ten in all, were mostly of views of bridges. They were of the greatest beauty. The Prime Minister took them to a specialist who confirmed that they were first issues. They were part of a series Hokusai had done about 1826 of bridges and waterfalls. They were worth a large sum of money.

The Prime Minister felt he could not accept them. He made up his mind to take them back to Madame de Vizille. But one

140

thing after another cropped up to delay his going and he was obliged in the end to send her a letter, saying that he would come at the earliest he could to bring the prints back to her, since they were, as she might not know, very valuable.

Three months later he saw the opportunity and fixed the date. Then one morning he had a letter from Paris. It was a lawyer's letter and enclosed a sealed note from Madame de Vizille which, said the letter, she had been unable to send on to him before she had died.

He opened it. It was written in a clear hand.

I know what they are. You are to keep them. I would like to think of you when you are older still having that charming humility of yours before great things and your good humour. You will find humility is despised and laughter often difficult. I have nobody else to teach. Hokusai will go on teaching you these things.

Three years had gone before he could visit Paris again. He went to the rue Payenne to look at the house. In the rue Pavée, just before he got there, he had a feeling he ought not to continue, and after hesitating, he turned back. He had inquired about the house and learned that it had been taken over by a firm of metal-furniture makers who had gutted it and rendered it hideous with plastic signs, metal windows and fluorescent lighting. He was glad he hadn't seen it. But the past and Madame de Vizille had been kept alive in all their beauty by the Hokusais and he still drew strength from the pictures.

The telephone rang. The Prime Minister opened his eyes. He seemed to have been a great distance away. In a second everything of the present had flooded into his mind again. But he felt refreshed and got up.

The door opened and Henning showed the Lord President in. The Lord President looked bowed and older. His tongue passed nervously over his lip several times.

'You've seen Messender?' he said.

The Prime Minister nodded. 'Yes.'

The Lord President's hands grasped the lapels of his coat. He planted his feet apart. He swayed from side to side. He gazed at the Prime Minister and deep seams furrowed his bloodhound face. 'I do not see how we can keep quiet any longer,' he said. 'Since you won't do what I advise, surely you can say that the Captain got off course, that it was a navigational error, that he was bound for the Pole and strayed into Soviet waters by mistake?'

They had been over all this. The Prime Minister saw that the Lord President had come to apply pressure.

'We agreed that that will not help.'

'Then I think the party has a right to expect that you admit your personal error and place yourself – place your future as Prime Minister and leader of the party – in its hands. At once. I may say that my Cabinet colleagues hold the same view.' The Lord President's eyes were fixed on the Prime Minister's.

Then that was it.

The Prime Minister felt a great sadness. He had refused to listen to the whisperings about the Lord President all these years. But they had apparently been true. He was being told to step down, acknowledge defeat and discredit, and leave the way open for the Lord President to snatch up the reins at this hour of crisis – since there could be no question of changing government at such a moment – and ride to power. But he could not believe there was a majority of the Cabinet against him.

'I shall account for myself to the party, Lord President,' he said. 'But first I shall account for my duty to the country. It is not my duty to resign at such a moment.'

Raspingly, the Lord President said, 'That is the echo of Neville Chamberlain in nineteen-forty when we were going headlong to disaster!'

'With the difference, Lord President, that you are not now our Winston Churchill.'

The Lord President flinched. He flung round with closed lips and marched to the window. He stood with his back to the Prime Minister. It was a feint. He was coming in again. When he turned, he said, 'And how do you intend accounting for the loss of the submarine?'

'I have not decided. I am awaiting a confidential report on

Russian air activity from our man at Omaha and one from the Ambassador in Moscow.'

'Once more, what is to prevent us announcing that the ship has been lost in the North Sea?'

'Nothing except that it does not answer the case. They may locate the submarine, for one thing, secure the secret orders and expose us.'

With clenched jaws, the Lord President said, 'We would swear they were forgeries.'

'And the submarine?'

'A masquerade! Look what the Chinese did with their germ-war campaign against Ridgway and the Americans.'

'No, no. It will not do. It would be infamous. We cannot do these things.'

'My God! To save the country? Would you not, Prime Minister, would you not commit a dozen infamies to stave off Russian rockets from this country?'

'You are asking me to run the risk of having Her Majesty's Government and the party branded internationally as liars and confounded with the proofs of their own duplicity.'

'A minimal risk.'

'The Russians may at this moment be preparing to announce that they have the submarine and fatally cut us off from American sympathy and help. They will design it to arouse American fury against us. That announcement, I am convinced, would be the preliminary to an attack on us and we shall go to final alert the instant they make it.'

The Lord President said, 'But they could not get the submarine up overnight! They could not get the proofs of our duplicity, as you call them, together fast enough. That is why I urge that we get in first, take the wind out of their sails.'

'They could sow doubt in the Americans' minds. Washington lately, as you know . . .'

'It is a gamble. But good God! We can *only* gamble now!'

The Prime Minister felt his mind being invaded by a fearful uncertainty. Should he yield to this argument? He wished he could believe it was entirely untramelled with other considerations.

143

But even now, he could not bring himself to attribute baser motives to the Lord President. He felt he was not succeeding in keeping his hesitation out of his face. The Lord President was ominously silent. Should he, after all, play this devious and dangerous game? It was the sort of course that Messender, as well as the Lord President, would take naturally. Were they right? Was he losing his touch, clinging too closely to the methods and principles of the past in a world where ruthlessness was the order of the day? He had once been accused by opponents of trying to behave 'like an eighteenth-century humanist' – and the gibe had aroused laughter. Then it might be that, after all, he was wrong.

He was unexpectedly startled by a knock on the door. They both turned. 'Come in.'

It was Henning. He was, the Prime Minister noticed, showing signs of strain. He handed the Prime Minister a sheet of paper. It was a personal hand message from the Minister of Defence. The Prime Minister unfolded it. As Henning left, shutting the door, he read out ' "The following signal was received from *Uranus* at 0522 hours. Begins Defence Ministry from *Uranus* ship was disabled by Communist saboteur who is among survivors ends." '

The Prime Minister looked up. He met the Lord President's hooded eyes. 'Then the chances that the Russians know, or will soon know, are increased. We cannot do what you suggest. We should be putting our heads into a noose; and saving nothing.'

The Lord President drew a deep breath. He sighed. Slowly he nodded his head and shoulders in what seemed like bows of resignation. 'Yours is the responsibility, Prime Minister,' he said in a low voice.

'That I accept,' the Prime Minister said. 'I have an old-fashioned conception of responsibility. But it is not inappropriate, since it is the conception they hold to in the Navy.

'Imagine for a moment that we were not under this terrible threat and were debating this issue in the House. I have no doubt that if I played the honest man abused, explained that I had been let down by expert and well-intentioned subordinates, even, to a certain extent, led astray, I have no doubt that we should, with a three-line whip, get away with it at the division. But where would my responsibility be?

'In the Navy, when the officer of the watch, perhaps a lieutenant, endangers the ship, the captain cannot dissociate himself from personal responsibility. His is the entire responsibility. He may have had no personal hand in the incident. However justified, he may not point to the lieutenant. He is responsible. Otherwise, why have a – why have a Prime Minister?'

Brusquely, the Lord President's head snapped up. 'You would resign?'

The Prime Minister said, 'I intend taking my responsibility to the limit.'

The telephone rang again. The Prime Minister answered, listened and said 'Yes, please.' The Lord President was staring moodily out of the window. The Prime Minister lit a cigarette. 'It is the report from Moscow,' he said.

The Defence Minister came in with Henning. Henning said, 'The Foreign Secretary is coming round with the report at once. He asked me to tell you that it gives the latest movements of certain Russians, but the main point is that Kruschev has not been seen now for thirty-six hours. It is fairly unusual. There was known to be a meeting of one of the Communist Party committees. They may be holding this somewhere outside Moscow, the Ambassador doesn't know. Marshal Mikulich, who was due to attend the Bolshoi ballet gala yesterday in honour of a Polish army delegation, unexpectedly did not turn up and has not been seen either.'

'My God!' the Lord President said from the window.

'It does not look good, does it?' the Defence Minister said. The Prime Minister looked at him inquiringly. The Defence Minister said, 'I have brought the new Yorkshire station into the Ballistic Missile Early Warning System. It is not yet working completely but it will help to give us a few moments' warning.'

CHAPTER TWELVE

THE COMBINED OPERATIONS ROOM at the Ministry of Defence, permanently manned, had been brought to full strength. It was underground. In the complex surrounding it were the separate Naval, Army and Air Force Operations Rooms which had been in the process of transferring underground from the building above when the crisis occurred. They too were now fully manned.

The three Chiefs of Staff and Montfalcon, who formed the combined central intelligence of the organization, sat in a separate sound-proof room, off the main Ops Room. It was furnished with four desks, each with three green-handled scrambler telephones and a bell-push, an electric fire and a spare table; that was all. When the Chiefs wished to consult a map they walked out into the adjoining Combined Ops Room. They summoned nobody to the sound-proof sanctum except messengers. It was a room for quiet, rapid thought with the minimum of error.

Outside, in the main Operations Room, there was a continuous unhurried activity. Officers moved from maps to tables. Code-words were being passed. Batteries of Telex machines were muttering and quiet voices spoke into telephones. There were none of the consoles and spectacular electronics of the Omaha War Room.

One end of the room was fitted with a brightly illuminated bay. From time to time orderlies pulled wall-sized charts, radar scanning overlays, maps and diagrams mounted on frames and overhead runners out under the lights for groups of officers to study. The charts carried magnetic symbols and coloured lights for ships, aircraft, tanks, troops, stores and a hundred other things. Elsewhere, charts and maps with other symbols were spread on tables.

The scene had all the signs of quiet efficiency. Yet to those

146

accustomed to observe these inner workings, there was a desperate unreality about it. Scarcely an officer in the room had detached himself sufficiently from the universal assumption that all this, once it happened, would be happening in company with the Americans and NATO, to take seriously the defence of England by England alone.

Everything was proceeding according to the contingency plan which had, of course, been ready – instantly ready. But it responded to a contingency which had not been believed in simply because at every turn it papered over hideous lacunae.

For years it had been a Ministry byword, 'a ring of the proud currency of independence', as the Minister had put it, that 'NATO can't declare war but Britain can'. There were officers now who saw that that was a dreadful consolation indeed. Much of the 'standard procedure' to meet a crisis was not under British jurisdiction at all and accordingly another byword had been that 'a lot goes on in an alert that is out of our hands because it's built that way'.

Four and a half minutes warning, which was what England could now expect, left no time for rebuilding. Soviet Golem missiles, fired from submarines off the East coast, would reduce the warning to two and a half minutes.

Petty Officer Punchard was sleeping. His sleep progressed in undulations with his snoring. The snore began small and fluttering, a mere dove-like beating of wings, grew to a steady sound and strengthened as Punchard's mouth opened wider, rose, and rose again to a sound like a hacksaw, then to a harsh metallic rasping, his mouth opening further and the snore becoming like the rattle of engine pistons until, with a blasting blare at the top, jaw dropped wide, mouth-edges vibrating, he choked, nearly woke, snapped his mouth shut over the snore as he stirred and in sudden silence coasted down to the trough of the wave and softly began fluttering up the next rise.

'Blimey, wish I could kip like that,' Tippett said.

'Think of all the air goin' in there,' Maxwell said.

'An' all the air comin' out poison.'

'He ain't using no more air than you or me,' Vickers said.

147

'I betcher he is. You can't snore like that without air.'

'Punch is all right, poor old sod.'

A pause.

'Can you sleep, Vick?'

'Not much.'

'I can't neither. What d'you think about?'

'Oh Christ, all sorts o' things.'

'Me too. Sometimes I think about all that water up there an' them steel plates, that's all that's keeping it off, an' I wonder what it's like if you could look up. Then I think about grub an' ... I dunno, a lot of funny things like getting your hair cut at Walton's, an' that pair of budgies they got in the Crown or ridin' in a tram. Funny 'n it?'

'Yes.'

'My old man use to like ridin' in trams too. 'E was funny. 'E use to pick them little ones with the open ends that use to do a switchback like from side to side. He use to say they sounded like dragons to 'im, comin' down the road, when they put the brakes on. You use to hear 'em comin' at night and they started to put the brakes on comin' down the hill towards the stop and they use to give a kind a roar or it was like a moan. And you could see my old man listenin'. He use to be readin' the paper an' 'is eye use to go off the print and 'e use to sort of smile to 'imself when he 'eard the old tram comin'. And when they put the brake on 'e use to like it, and grin to 'imself a bit harder, and still not be readin' the paper. 'E use to read Captain Coe. Then after the tram had stopped and was going off again, it use to go down the road and he use to be listenin' and he knew when it was just passin' the police station and the Red Lion and the driver use to stamp on the bell they had and it use to go *ting-ting, ting-ting* faint like and my old man use to be grinnin' like mad to 'imself. And then you couldn't hear the tram any more and he use to turn back to Captain Coe, or maybe it was Faughaballah.'

'Yes?'

'What was your old man like, Vick?'

'He's still alive, the old so-and-so. Suppose he's all right. He married again, after the old woman pegged out. I could

148

never get on with the new one.'

'Funny 'n it?'

'Yes.'

Punchard crested a snore, choked, shifted his position. The trough was deeper than usual and the silence lasted a little longer.

'You know what I'd like, Vick?'

'What?'

'A bloody great woman. Pass the time like. Ha-ha. One with tits like balloons, eh?'

'That's it.'

'You seen that dark bit in the shop next to the Anchor? No? She's all right.'

'Oh, you mean in the newsagent's? She's called Pat.'

'You sound well in.'

'No. I wouldn't mind though.'

'D'you reckon she would?'

'I dunno. No harm trying.'

'I see her in the saloon bar one evenin'. She come in with another girl. I thought a minute I'd go round, you know, but they got talkin' to some chap. I seen him before, he's a furniture salesman. I thought if I go round and start talkin' to 'em I can see her givin' me the old look, you know, oh a bloody sailor an' 'e smells of beer and don't let's go with 'im Daise 'n the fellow saying to 'em "I got the old MG outside, let's go up the road'ouse." You know.'

'Yes.'

A pause. 'We got to have another go at getting those poor sods out next door.'

'As soon as Punch's awake.'

A long silence.

'Vick?'

'Uh?'

'What day is it?'

'I dunno. Wednesday. Maybe, I dunno.'

'I reckon it's Friday. You know, I was thinkin'.'

'What?'

'It's like being nowhere. I mean it's like when you're on

149

watch at the reactor compartment, just sittin' watchin' the dials hour after hour. The dials keep on gettin' bigger and bigger. Sometimes you don't even feel yourself givin' the crank a turn, everything's a dial, like you're a dial and you don't exist.'

'I know.'

'Listen, you can't hear the scrub.'

'It's Punchard. He's the bloody scrub.'

'I mean, we ain't moving or rollin' a little bit because we ain't in the water, Vick. I keep feelin' we're under the mud – the whole six-thousand-odd tons of us. You know, we been sinkin' and then siltin' up and it's covered all over us.'

'Couldn't do yet.'

'If there's a big tow like the Old Man said?'

'Not even.'

'Do you reckon that was right about them gettin' a signal away? I mean, was they just sayin' that?'

'I should think it went. Christ, old Punch is going to choke himself with his false teeth in a minute.'

Conditions had worsened for the eight men in the torpedo compartment and the crew's mess. The scrubber, now manifestly defective, was still pumping out the CO_2 but the system was failing to 'bleed' in oxygen at a steady rhythm. Bosco and Green were working on two valves of the bleed system where the piping connected with an input farther aft. It seemed that a leakage was occurring somewhere fairly close to, which would interfere with the pressure and cause the erratic behaviour.

The emergency light, run on batteries, was dimming too. With no motive power, they had no means of recharging. The temperature in both compartments had risen. All the men were stripped to the minimum and they all had stubble on their chins.

Fitch came in from the torpedo compartment. Haynes and Cubit were talking together at the far table. Fitch went over.

'Listen, Dave, for Christ's sake, I've had this.'

Haynes looked at Cubit.

'That scrubber's not going to last much longer.'

'And we're going to be in the dark before long.'

From the other side of the mess Robertson said, 'There's a part-used portable light in the torpedo room.'

'Where from?' Fitch said, pugnaciously. 'I never seen it.'

'I saved it.'

'Well,' Cubit smiled sarcastically. 'Our hero. Ginger, see he gets a mention in dispatches.'

'Next time the dispatches go, Fitch,' Haynes said.

Fitch said impatiently, 'For Christ's sake, what do we do? The escape gear's there. If we don't go soon we're not going to have the chance.'

'Fitch, you know the orders,' Robertson said. 'If you try to —'

'Ah, shut up, Robertson,' Haynes said, vaguely. 'You want to stay – stay!'

'Haynes, I've had about enough of your lip.'

'Then shut up!'

'I'll smash you!'

'We're not asking you.'

'Do what you like, Robertson.'

The others were on their feet at once. They stood bristling at Robertson. Bosco jumped down from the stool and came over. Cubit's eyes went over Robertson's shoulder to Wingrove's bulky form blocking the doorway to the torpedo room. But before Wingrove could intervene, Robertson turned away. He took two paces, then turned round to face them. 'We'll settle it later, Haynes – and good.' He jerked his head to Wingrove. Wingrove came in and they sat down at the far table.

The rest grouped round Haynes.

'Careful what you say, boys, Copper Robertson's listening,' Cubit said, grinning. He touched his sore lips.

'Wait till you get to Moscow, Cubit, the land o' the free,' Robertson said, 'where they don't have coppers.'

'Ha ha,' Cubit said.

'For Christ's sake! What do we do?' Fitch said.

Haynes said, 'You want to go, Ginger? Go. Who's stopping you?' Fitch made a movement of impatience. 'Depends if you believe there's that current up there or not, doesn't it?'

'I reckon that's a lot of bull just to keep us down here,' Fitch said.

Haynes shrugged. 'Could be. Only it's a chance you've got to take, isn't it? You won't find out till you're out there and then it'll be too late to change your mind.'

Cubit was grinning. 'You don't think the Royal Navy is coming here to rescue you, do you, Ginge?'

'Eh?' Bosco said, frowning. He had abandoned work on the scrubber. Green was still at it. 'Why not?'

'Good Christ, Bosco does too! They think there's MTBs, rescue tugs and a couple of cruisers all steaming here hell for leather and a few helicopters circling overhead right now at X marks the spot. Eh, Fitch?'

Green looked round listening. He stopped work and came over. Fitch said nothing.

'They're stirring a hot grog up there for you already,' Cubit said.

'They must be doing something – they're . . . Do you mean to say they're not —?'

'It stands to reason they can't come in this close, man,' Haynes said. 'It'd have to be a bloody coastal raid.'

'But the Old Man said —'

'He said! He said "something" was going to be done. Something – you know. It's typical. Something'll turn up. In the meantime, we can all pass out.'

'What are you waiting for then?' Fitch said.

Haynes leant forward, chin on hand. 'If you want to know, I've been expecting the Russians. If anybody's going to get us out of this, they are, whether we like it or not.'

'Why ain't they turned up then, if they're so bloody smart?' Green said.

'Shut up, Greeny,' Bosco said.

'No, Greeny's right,' Cubit said. 'We don't know why they haven't. Maybe they're watching to see what we're going to do. But I'll tell you something, all of you; make you a proposition. If you like I'll go and bring 'em.'

Movement stopped. They all looked at him, surprised.

152

Robertson thought Haynes's surprise was put on. Haynes's eyes were quickly observing the others.

'Not on your life,' Green said. 'You'd leave us all to go to hell.'

'Sure he would!' Robertson called out. 'Or get the Russians to come and finish us.'

'Who asked you?' Fitch said.

'Are they waiting specially for you?'

'Yes, what makes you so sure you'd be picked up?' Bosco said.

'I'm not sure. I'm willing to take a chance, that's all,' Cubit said. 'If any of you try and you make it, you'll be snitched. I can make the Russians listen to me.'

Fitch made a face. He obviously didn't much like the idea. Bosco seemed to be waiting for a lead.

Cubit said, 'Look, if you don't believe me, if you think I'm going to save my own skin, why don't you send somebody with me? Wingrove, for instance?'

They thought about this, looked at each other.

'You'd twist it at the last minute,' Robertson said. 'What'd stop you telling your Russian pals that Wingrove's a bastard?'

'All right. So you've got everything to lose. You just sit here and pass out, or wait till they come and do you.'

Fitch said to Haynes, 'Shall we, Dave?'

Haynes looked round from face to face. 'Could do worse.'

Robertson made a sound of disgust and turned his back, then he suddenly swung round again. 'If you bring the Russians to this ship, you're delivering the ship into enemy hands. That's a crime, Cubit – it's bloody treason! And I'll shop you for it.'

'If you get the chance,' Cubit said. 'Don't make me laugh.' He swelled with self-assurance. 'Who's the enemy? Who's the aggressor? Entering a country's territorial waters is invasion. Do you hear, Petty Officer Robertson? Invasion!'

He turned to Haynes. 'Am I right?'

'Right,' Haynes said.

'Trust the sea lawyer,' Robertson said.

'Get back to work, Greeny,' Fitch said. Green got up reluctantly and went back to the scrubber connection.

Cubit bent forward and the others leaned in towards him. In a low voice, Cubit said, 'We'll wait and pick the right moment; and we don't tell the Old Man about this. Understand?'

'Right,' Haynes said. The others nodded.

Cubit sat back. In a louder tone he said, 'We're just being sacrificed, that's all.'

'Sacrificed for your country!' Robertson said.

'Sure,' Haynes said. 'It's sacrifice when you do what they tell you. Otherwise, you're a bastard. A lot of hypocritical bull. Who are we to be pushed around any longer by the bloody politicians and the managers and the aristocracy and their stately homes where you can meet all the very top people? They think they've got a segregation problem in America. Ours isn't even racial segregation, it's segregation of the same bloody race. Go to a snob school and you buy your ticket to run England – or your old man buys it. One of our top people. If you're not one of our top people, boy, you're just a load o' —. We're an affluent society, they tell you – society's the trick word now, everything's a something society. But if you're a bloody fool and you can't compete on ordinary terms, it doesn't make any difference as long as you can pay. You got the right to spit on other people. You're a natural-born manager for life because your old man's got the money. You go to Eton and Oxford and you get a commission in the Guards and a partnership in the City and you move among the top people. You never meet anybody but the top people and *they* know you're one of the top people, because you've got the cash and your accent's all right and you've got the right attitude about the top people and the lower orders, whom you don't have to meet.

'So here we are, HMS *Uranus* being run by the top people. Don't take any notice of me, Robertson, I'm only a naval rating. But I got brains enough to see that this is a cock-up, haven't you?

'You know what, Robbie? I had a job in the Ministry of Transport once. It was temporary and the Ministry of Transport is nothing world-shaking. But I used to think I didn't

154

know anything. I had the idea it wasn't any good me thinking that things were a balls-up – I could see they were – because the bosses and the top political boys knew what was what. They knew a lot more that I didn't know. They had all the answers.

'After eighteen months I didn't think so any more. I found out there were a lot of bloody fools. Then I found out it didn't matter, their being bloody fools. They wouldn't have made POs on their merits. They fumbled and farted around and they got away with it because they were all With It, as they say. Oh, by Christ, they were With It all right.

'They like to keep you talking about the social revolution that's supposed to have come over the British Isles. The great Silent Revolution and social justice and all that, all brought on by the war. But all the war did was to push a lot of new people into the money. It didn't change the rules! The top people! When I see that look on their faces when they hear an accent they don't like, I tell you I want to – I want to wipe 'em off the face of the earth, boy. You hear 'em with their loud arrogant bloody voices. You'd think it was *time* for a revolution to finish the bastards all off. Oh, but not on your life! Everybody falls in with the bloody thing – kowtowing to the Great English Segregation Movement. They lap it up! *They* want to segregate somebody else – the man below!

'You hear the young marrieds in the suburbs, learning the right "smart" phrases. They've got the vogue words in the vogue order and if Whosit says it's Non-U, oh Christ, you have to be careful or people might think your mum wasn't the Duchess of Whatsit but only her skivvy. A load o' snobbery, English life. "I'm better than you, Ted, because I eat with a fish-knife or I don't eat with a fish-knife." They get a snob attitude out of anything – what you eat, what you wear, how you wear it, who you know, where you go, anything! You imagine asking for military pickle in a West-End pub? East o' Bow Station, mate, kindly. Get back to your High-talian caffs. They're all running around looking for bits of snobbery like they were looking for gold. They live on snobbery. The great English game – how to show you're one of the Right People and kick down the ones below. Yah! And Robertson's their prophet.'

Robertson got up and walked into the torpedo room. Wingrove stayed where he was, looking at Cubit.

Davis held a small piece of cardboard, an unfolded cigarette packet, on his knee, squatting with legs drawn up and his back against part of the engine casing. He was staring unseeingly at the cardboard. He sat quite still, breathing shallowly. Petty Officer Punchard left the men working on the jammed watertight door, came over and sat beside him.

'Ain't you going to finish the letter, Fred?'

Davis seemed to hear indistinctly. He turned his head vaguely in the opposite direction, then round to Punchard.

'Eh?'

'I said, finish your letter up, lad.' Punchard had noticed his growing abstraction and suggested he write a letter to his wife 'so she'll have news straight off, soon as we get out'.

'What's the use, Punch?'

'Course there's use. I told you. It's always twenty-four hours before you can get out of barracks away on survivor's leave. Get it posted first thing ashore and she'll have it already, see?'

Davis didn't seem to have listened very closely. He was watching a bluebottle on his leg. The bluebottle had mysteriously appeared in the compartment an hour before. .

'Wonder where it's been?' Davis said.

'Where do flies go in the winter-time?' Punchard said, then laughed. 'That reminds me. Did I ever tell you about the time we put into the Seychelles in *Scorpion*? I didn't? When we'd been on exercises with the Americans and the Commander, old Dizzy Duxton, gave the port watch leave? Stone the crows, what a night!'

He launched into a long and circumstantial saga, watching Davis's face and trying to keep his attention on the story. Davis nodded once or twice, answered Punchard's rhetorical questions mechanically. Punchard finished with a chuckle.

There was a short silence. Davis was staring at the deck

plating. 'Punch, I can smell cooking fat.'

'Come off it, Fred.'

'I can.'

'What they cookin', pound o' pork sausages?'

Davis shook his head. He raised his eyes and looked across the compartment. 'If you could see a bit farther off. If you could see not just fifteen foot in front of you all the time. If you could see a chimney-pot or a tree.' Suddenly he shouted 'Miles and miles and bloody miles – out of here!'

The others looked round. Then, as Punchard gripped his arm, he broke off, jabbing his fist into his cheek.

'All right, boy,' Punchard said. 'Here, have a fag-end.'

CHAPTER THIRTEEN

THE PRIME MINISTER had a small room at the Ministry of Defence. He had endowed it with a certain symbolism. It was windowless, soundproofed, barely furnished with desk, upright chairs, standard lamp and dark grey carpet. The walls were painted grey and they were bare. There were no papers on the desk, nothing but one note-pad, ashtray and one telephone. At one time, the Prime Minister had thought of putting a single Hokusai print on the wall, but he had not been able to bring himself to it.

The Prime Minister hated the room. It filled him with despair. He had never entered it, on the air-raid exercises which he and the members of the government had gone through periodically, without feeling that it did, indeed, symbolize the very end of things.

The Prime Minister had been sitting at the desk for twenty minutes. Twice he had risen and taken a few paces up and down the room and then resumed his seat. He had allowed himself half an hour to reach a final decision. He had just come to this decision and sent for Montfalcon. He was calm and outwardly at ease.

The light from the standard lamp showed a faint shimmer of greying stubble on his chin. He had had no time to shave since his early-morning visit to the Sovereign. He had realized with a small shock, running his hand over his chin as the car drove into the Palace courtyard, that he had forgotten. He had taken no time to go up to his personal rooms in Number 10 before setting out, only too relieved that the royal family were readily accessible and not in Scotland. In some ways he wished they were abroad in the Dominions at this critical hour. But he knew they would feel otherwise.

At the interview he had adopted a Churchillian line and

simply advised the Sovereign that he was taking over as Minister of Defence. There would be no legislation.

As he stubbed out his cigarette, the door opened without a preliminary knock and Montfalcon came in. He shut the door behind him.

The Prime Minister rose and stepped round the desk.

'John, this thing is not to be resolved without a hideous risk. But I have made up my mind.'

Montfalcon stood looking at him without a flicker. It was a cold face, the Prime Minister couldn't help thinking. But that jagged profile, the bloodless skin and the bearing of almost imperial pride expressed great energy. There was also the peculiar ruthlessness of the man of arms. The Prime Minister had often wondered what Montfalcon's destiny would have been if he had not been born an Englishman. He could easily see him, with those icy eyes, leading a *coup d'état*.

'The submarine must be destroyed.'

'And we say nothing?' Montfalcon said.

'We say nothing. The Russians could not mistake the wreckage of the submarine for a threat, for a stealthy attack. Nor could they, I think, use it effectively with the United States against us. What's more, we should be destroying the secret gear. Once the thing was done, I should find an opportunity of telling the President.'

'You are thinking, I take it, of attacking with another submarine?'

'Yes.' The Prime Minister had suddenly become tense. 'To send a second submarine — it hardly bears thinking of. It doubles the risk. But I can't see any other way.'

'And what of the men?'

There was an agonized moment of silence. The unspoken words hung between them. All the outrage of ordering Montfalcon to send British seamen to fire on other British seamen was present in the Prime Minister's mind. Yet the supreme interests of the country were at stake. He believed that because of this, Montfalcon would carry out the orders. Nevertheless, it would be intolerable, he felt, to make it explicit, to put it into words to the Air Marshal.

This was the final decision which the Prime Minister had found so hard to take. There had been occasions in the past when British serving men had killed each other. But they had been accidents, mistakes – at the best merciful killings of men who were doomed in any event. But to send men in cold blood to kill others waiting for rescue! They could not, of course, be told what they were going to do. Yet this almost compounded the evil of it. It was atrocious, yet inescapable.

The Lord President's words about resigning had come to the Prime Minister as he had wrestled with the alternatives. How simple! How enviable a course! Harry Truman, he remembered, had kept a little notice on his desk at the White House: The Buck Stops Here.

He took a deep breath. This was a personal version of the moment known in Whitehall jargon as 'the crunch'.

'Is there any possible way of saving them?'

Montfalcon barely moved. His eyes strayed briefly to one or two points in the room, then returned to the Prime Minister's. 'If we timed the survivors' escape for the second submarine's arrival, it might pick them up.'

'But that would mean informing it in advance that there were men alive in *Uranus*.'

'It would.'

'And telling the survivors that we were attempting to rescue them. That would make it impossible to order the second submarine to destroy *Uranus* with torpedoes.'

'There is a self-destruction device in *Uranus* which is meant to prevent the secret equipment falling into enemy hands and will largely wreck the ship if it is operated. It works on a time fuse. There are two of the devices, in fact, if they can be reached.'

The Prime Minister was looking intently into Montfalcon's face. He seemed to catch a gleam of hope. 'Could we not try to get the men out and then use these demolition charges?'

Except for a slight tensing of the lips, Montfalcon's face did not change. 'It might be done.'

'Then we must try to do it.'

'That is your decision, Prime Minister?'

160

'Yes. But the submarine must be destroyed.'

'Will you kindly come to the Ops Room?' Montfalcon said. They took a step towards the door. The Prime Minister said, 'The thing is, can it be done in time?'

'We already have a submarine approaching the north of Norway.'

'What!' The Prime Minister stopped at the door in surprise.

'It's normal war station under the alert, Prime Minister.'

The Prime Minister searched Montfalcon's face. Was there a fugitive gleam of something else in the eyes – defiance?

'Then she can be used?'

'She has been sent for use – once the political decision was taken.' It sounded bizarre; yet there was a hint of reparation in the words. Was Montfalcon saying that they had made a mistake – 'they' of the non-political world who were supposed to exist only by virtue of the political leaders but who had been moving into more and more powerful positions in all the nations of the world – and now had made their arrangements to rectify it 'once the political decision was taken'?

'She can reach the area quickly,' Montfalcon was saying. 'She is a large conventional submarine with schnorkel and long-range sonar and will therefore be able to detect the Russians if they are on the spot – if they don't detect her first.'

'If she suspects they're there, she must retire and we will have to meet the situation as best we can.'

Montfalcon opened the door and they went out into the corridor. They turned left, passed the guard of Royal Marines and entered the Combined Operations Room.

Activity had increased, the pitch was higher. But there was the same cool control in all the movements and voices. Heads were raised here and there as the Prime Minister and Montfalcon came in, then lowered again. There was not more than mild curiosity. On the far side, the First Sea Lord and the Chief of Air Staff were standing in front of a wall chart surrounded by a group of other officers. The officers moved aside as the Prime Minister and Montfalcon came up.

Montfalcon spoke. 'The Prime Minister has decided that

Uranus must be destroyed, a decision in which I concur. I have explained that she carries demolition charges which will destroy her and the Prime Minister has agreed that we should first endeavour to rescue the survivors, giving them orders to set the demolition charges to explode after they have left the ship. The alternative is to destroy *Uranus* by torpedo attack. I propose we discuss the first course. I have told the Prime Minister that it is possible by sending *Stingray* from the station she is now taking up north of Norway.'

There was a murmur, a shifting in the group. They all turned to the chart and there was a general exchange.

The First Sea Lord was obviously worried and ill at ease.

'As I say, I see no difficulty about moving *Stingray* down there. She has enough diving endurance. But it's going to be very trickly getting her in precisely the spot at precisely the moment the survivors come up. It's a matter of landing on a pinpoint. There might be a small error in the position *Uranus* has given us which would make all the difference. Sonar will help, of course, but there would have to be high accuracy in getting to the position at exactly the right time.'

The Prime Minister said, 'I take it you would synchronize the two ship's clocks. But there should be no reason why you shouldn't signal *Stingray*'s position every so often to *Uranus* – give her news of the approach, so to speak, as you give her a check on the time.'

'*Stingray* would be silent, sir,' the Signals Officer said.

The First Sea Lord said, 'And you see, when she got there she wouldn't be a good vantage point. A submarine on the surface has a low profile and a conventional submarine like *Stingray* is lower than a nuclear submarine. Unless she is dead on the pinpoint, it is going to be very hard for her to spot anything or for the survivors to spot her.'

'Yes.' They considered this. At last the Prime Minister said, 'Where are the controls of the demolition charges?'

Nobody knew offhand. There was a consultation and after some hasty reference to a plan, an officer produced the answer. One in the control room and one aft.

The Prime Minister said, 'If the time switches are not work-

162

ing, I take it the artificers will be able to rig a time fuse of some sort so that she is destroyed once they have left?'

'It depends on what tools and so forth they can get at, but if there is a minimum of gear we can expect it.'

The Director of Naval Operations intervened. 'With respect, I think we're forgetting that the position is within sight of the Russian shore!' He spoke forcefully. '*Stingray* would have to go in submerged. She could only surface for a very short time in darkness or at first light. There couldn't be any question of her cruising round looking for survivors. I don't like it at all. She'd have to give herself a few minutes, pick up whoever she could find, then dive and get the hell out of it fast. It's extremely dangerous. I make no bones about it; I detest the whole thing.'

'So we observe,' the Prime Minister said coldly.

An awkward silence followed.

'Whether the hull is demolished or not, there may be bodies drifting ashore,' the First Sea Lord said.

'Yes, I realize that,' the Prime Minister nodded. 'We can't avoid that, whatever we do. We shall have to prepare some explanation. After all, bodies do drift up all over the world.'

There was another awkward pause. Nobody seemed willing to speak. The Prime Minister caught the general feeling that a decision had not been made. Firmly he said, 'I consider that if the thing is feasible, we must attempt it.'

The officers exchanged glances.

'Any objections?' the First Sea Lord said.

'I dislike it – very much,' the Director of Operations said.

'We all do, Captain.' The Prime Minister was terse.

'Very well,' the First Sea Lord said. 'We shall signal *Uranus* what we intend and tell her to stand by.'

'Please do so,' the Prime Minister said.

Then it was settled. They were standing there preliminary to dispersal.

'Anything else?' the First Sea Lord said.

'Yes,' the Director of Naval Operations said. His face was drawn and angry. 'We have not dealt with the second alternative. If, for some reason that we do not know of, the demolition charges are inaccessible or cannot be blown, what are *Stingray*'s orders to be?'

The Prime Minister braced himself. He opened his mouth to answer. Suddenly Montfalcon said, 'You will send a signal to *Uranus* asking if the charges can be blown. If the answer is no, *Stingray* is to be told to go in and destroy the ship.'

'And the survivors?'

'There will be no survivors, Captain.'

CHAPTER FOURTEEN

JASON BENT TENSELY over the chart table, shifting the folded slip of paper along to the last cipher group of the signal. He looked up the word, wrote it on the pad. His hand left a wet mark on the paper. Impatiently he lifted his arm, wiping the sweat off his forehead. He flipped the cipher books shut and got up. He passed his hand over his eyes. It had taken him an hour and a half, working singlehanded, to decipher the long signal detailing the rescue operation.

The light in the compartment was weaker and it had become very hot. The scrubber was obviously failing. Connor and Bailey, like the men, were sleeping more and complaining that they woke with headaches. The situation was the same in the other compartments.

Jason reached for the log and entered the time of the signal and its general import. Hours before, he had sent a three-word reply to the Ministry's signal asking if the submarine's demolition charges could be blown: *Affirmative central charge*.

Jason felt greatly keyed up. Hitherto it had needed an increasing effort of will to stay alert. He had had to drive himself to simple tasks like deciphering or enciphering signals and entering the log. But now the signal of the rescue attempt had eliminated all that.

He studied the signal with a sort of grim incredulous resolve. It gave a schedule of time-checks and positions for which they would have to listen. He wrote down the times for the radio watch-keepers and tore the sheet off the pad. *Stingray* had started for their position several hours earlier.

Jason had decided already not to tell the crew. It was the one heartening thing they needed; but a hitch, once they had been filled with expectancy, would be so much worse – and the rescue operation was obviously full of risk. He must tell

Connor at once. *Stingray* was well on the way already! If there was no failure and everything went to plan they would put everybody through escape drill just before she arrived.

Jason put the signal in the drawer and moved to the ladder. Connor was sleeping above. Let him have it out for a few minutes longer, Jason thought. He grasped the ladder and went down. The men were lying about in exhausted attitudes on the long seat, on the wardroom table and the deck, most of them sleeping. Since the disaster he had felt a growing affinity with them; sometimes he had believed this was strictly the product of their circumstances and meant no healing of his disability. Yet he felt there had been a change within himself.

Kirby was on watch in the radio recess, reading a dog-eared and filthy paper-back. Jason gave him the schedule of time-checks and explained that the signals were to be listened for and the clock checked with them to the second. He said nothing about rescue.

'That's a damn fine beard you've got coming on there, Jock.'

'Like Landru, sir, that French feller,' Kirby said in his broad Scots. 'Just reading about him.'

'Everything all right?'

'Aye, sir.'

He turned back into the wardroom. MacFall got to his feet by the long seat on which they had laid Trimmer. Jason went over softly, stepping over the sleeping men.

MacFall gestured to Trimmer. 'I think he's about done, sir.'

Jason bent beside the seat. Trimmer was lying on his back, his eyes not quite shut. Jason felt the weak pulse. He said, 'Trimmer?'

No answer.

'Is there anything I can do?'

Trimmer didn't stir. Jason lifted the eyelid. The pupil was very small. He looked up at MacFall. 'Has he had morphine?'

MacFall nodded. 'We gave him a wallop.'

'Good man.'

'Poor sod, sir. He's got four kids, all boys.'

'How many have you got?'

'Me, sir? I only got one. Another one coming up next month.'

Jason said softly, 'I hope you'll be there to see it.'

MacFall said nothing.

'If he comes out of it, let me know. Wake me up if you have to. Anyway he's not in pain.'

'I'll be stayin' by him, sir.'

'All right. Good night.'

'Good night, sir.'

Jason went up to wake Connor.

Grimble was awakened by the pain of his leg. The light seemed dimmer. He was lying on his good side facing the bulkhead. He could hear the sounds and the voices of Punchard's men working at the jammed door. They had managed to open it another inch but now it seemed firmly fixed again. The gap was still too narrow to squeeze through. Beale had stopped giving any help.

Grimble shifted uneasily. He looked across the compartment. Beale had switched off the usual emergency light they used and turned on the second, which made the compartment more shadowy. He saw Beale sitting on the gear casing next to the demolition mechanism. He was staring into the panel where the time setting was made.

Beale had become more and more withdrawn. He hardly left the place by the demolition gear. He sat without speaking, taking no notice of Grimble's exchanges with Punchard and the others. Grimble knew he had broken the sealed wire on the demolition handle. He wasn't sure whether Beale knew how to set the thing. He had thought of telling Punchard. But Punchard would call out admonitions to him. It might tip the balance.

Grimble lay back and shut his eyes. He felt too exhausted to crawl to the door. His leg was worse and now swelling. They were making more noise at the door than usual. Punchard was giving directions and the others were all talking at once. He heard Punchard say, 'Now!' – they all stopped speaking.

There was a heavy grinding followed by a shout. He lifted his head and saw somebody squeezing through the gap in the doorway. The next minute Punchard was bending over him. 'Well, Lofty me old cock-sparrer, we did it, eh?'

Urgently, in a whisper, Grimble said, 'Go easy with Beale.'

Two or three others had come through into the compartment. Punchard turned. Vickers and Tippett were talking to Beale. Punchard went over. As they stood grouped there, Grimble saw Beale grip the red handle.

'Sure, sure . . .' Punchard was saying, nodding his head. Then they all went through into the other compartment. Vickers and Maxwell came in and carried Grimble to the door and helped him through. He saw Beale in the corner with Tippett and Davis. Punchard said something to Vickers and went to the phone.

'Captain, sir? PO Punchard. We've just got it open, sir, and brought them through with us.'

'Well done, Punchard,' Jason said. 'How are they?'

'Not too dusty, sir. We'll see after them.'

'PO Punchard, keep their spirits up, all of them. We shan't be much longer, I hope.'

'Aye, aye, sir.'

In the control room, Jason rang off. He turned to the radio recess. Kirby had just finished taking a signal. 'Have you got that time-check?' Jason said.

Kirby handed him the signal. The ship's time corresponded: *Stingray*'s position was now fast closing in. Anxiously Jason reminded himself that it was only a theoretical position given by the Ministry of Defence since *Stingray* herself was silent. But it could not go wrong now!

He felt a nervous tension which he had not experienced for years. Standing with the signal in his hand, he had a flash of panic at the thought of ultimate failure and he knew that, in a strange way, this was bound up with his relationship to the survivors, his own deepest feelings.

The time was 0045 hours. They had two hours thirty minutes more to wait.

Jason wiped the sweat off and climbed the ladder.

Green was leaning against the doorway of the torpedo compartment looking in at Wingrove. 'What's the matter with him?'

'Just flaked out,' Petty Officer Robertson said. He had stretched Wingrove out on the deck aft of the tubes and was sitting by him.

From the mess, Cubit called out, 'Good riddance.'

'Come here, Green,' Haynes said. Green turned and went over. Haynes jerked his head for Green to sit down. Fitch and Bosco were already at the table with Haynes and Cubit.

'What's up?' Green said. 'I'm going to kip. What you all doin'?'

It was 0050 hours.

'Sit down,' Haynes said harshly. He turned to Savage lying alongside and stirred him with his foot. Savage woke up. He rose and came to the table too.

They were all sweating and most of them breathing through their mouths. The single light burning left the rest of the compartment in shadow. Cubit looked round at them. 'Haynes and me are giving you a chance, all of you. If you've got any sense you'll take it. That scrubber's going. If we don't get out of this quick we're never going to get out.'

'Christ, ain't I been saying —'

'Shut up, Fitch,' Haynes said.

Cubit was in a state of cold anger. 'Look, Fitch, get it straight, we're running this. It's going to be no bloody game going up there with nobody waiting for us. The Old Man's going to do it our way.'

'What, our way?'

'We're going to make him call the Russians.'

'Call the —?'

'Do you want to get out or don't you?' Haynes said. 'If you do, *listen*!'

'But he'll never play.'

'Shut up, Fitch, for Christ's sake.'

They looked at each other. Quietly Bosco said, 'All right, so what do we do?'

Cubit said, 'You know something, Bosco? You've got no

sense. You see that buoy connection when you were working on the scrubber?'

'Buoy connection?'

'Jesus.' Cubit glanced at Haynes. 'About a foot from those two scrub valves, if you'd taken the trouble to look. That yellow panel with ABR 9X on it. If you don't know what that is, I'll tell you. The ABR —'

'Is the marker buoy,' Bosco said.

'Right. Not released.'

'How could it be? We'd most likely have been spotted by now if it had been.'

'Top marks again, Bosco.'

'What you getting so cocky about then?'

'Only that you can release it from that panel, Bosco.'

'What? You mean you can —?' Fitch swung round and looked across at the panel.

Green said, 'You wouldn't have come across it if you hadn't been pokin' at what we been doing on those valves.'

'We found it, didn't we?' Cubit said.

Haynes said, 'Listen, Bosco, you know how that buoy works?'

The buoy was meant to mark the spot for rescuers if the submarine met with an accident on a dive. Brightly painted and easily visible from a distance, it was automatically released if the submarine went down with any of the normal hull openings left open. When the submarine dived and the panel showing that all hull openings were shut was working correctly, the buoy was automatically switched over to the captive position and was not released. It was a section of this control line to the buoy that Cubit and Haynes had come across.

'All we got to do is to knock out that linchpin and up she goes,' Haynes said.

'I'll tell you something more, Bosco,' Cubit said. '*Now* we know what those dockside mateys were doing before we sailed. They put a check on it so that the buoy couldn't go up by accident.'

'How do you know?'

'I don't know. It stands to reason, though, otherwise the

170

buoy would be up. The Ministry of Defence knew we were coming into Russian waters.'

'You don't know for certain that it ain't up,' Green said.

'For God's sake, Greeny,' Fitch said.

'But the Russians might know we was here already and just be watchin', playin' with us. Cubit said so, didn't he?'

'If they thought we were just lying on the bottom and they didn't know what we were up to, they would,' Cubit said. 'But not with a marker buoy up. They'd investigate.'

'Yes. Blow us all to cat's-meat,' Savage said.

'God almighty!' Haynes said. 'This ship's a prize packet, boy. Look at the gear there's here! They're going to try to raise her, or at least fish some of the stuff out. But by that time, you, me and the rest of us are just going to be corpses.'

'If they've put a check on the buoy, it won't go up now, will it?' Bosco said.

Cubit nodded. 'It will. Those dockside mates weren't working this far along the connection. Anyway, we've got other means.'

Haynes made a movement of impatience. 'I'm not arguing the toss any more. We're all in it and that's how it is. Anybody who wants to quit can fall out and join Robertson. Right?'

His eyes went from face to face. Nobody spoke. Haynes jerked his head to Cubit. Cubit got up and went to the intercom. He rang the bridge. They sat immobile, watching him.

Jason's voice came over. 'Bridge. Captain.'

'Listen, Lieutenant-Commander Jason, Royal Navy, this is Leading ME Cubit, ex-Royal Navy speaking. We have something to tell you and you'd better get cracking, see? We —'

Jason cut in, 'Put Petty Officer Fitch on, at once!'

'Don't "at once" me, Lieutenant-Commander Jason. Petty Officer Fitch is with me and we are all saying this to you —'

'Drop that tone, Cubit! What in God's name do you think you're up to? Put Fitch on immediately.'

'We're not going to get anywhere if you blow your top – *sir*,' Cubit said. 'We have a very interesting proposition to make to you.'

'Cubit, for the last time, I am warning you. You are guilty

of insolence and insubordination to your commanding officer. I am logging you and you will do as I say!'

Cubit held the phone away from his face. He blew a raspberry. Then he spoke into the mouthpiece again. 'Listen, Jason, we're in command in this section and we're going to stay in command. That means Fitch too. *We* are telling you! We're telling you that we are sending up the marker buoy *at once*, do you hear, Jason, at once, unless you send out a radio SOS to the Russians with our position. Get it?'

There was a pause. Then Jason's voice said tensely and quietly, 'Have you gone mad?'

'Do you get it, Jason? Don't ring off because the minute you do, that buoy's going up. You know we can do it. We've got the connection here.'

'Do you think, my man, that I'm going to submit to Communist blackmail? You are a criminal saboteur, responsible for the deaths of eighty shipmates —'

'"My man!" By Christ! Listen to one of our top people! What year d'you think you're living in?'

The line clicked. Jason had rung off.

Cubit and Haynes exchanged looks. 'Wait a minute and give him another go,' Haynes said.

They waited ten minutes then Cubit rang again.

'You try to settle it by ringing off?' Cubit said. 'Not very intelligent, Jason – and weak-minded.'

Jason said, 'I want to understand this clearly. You are asking me to send radio signals of our position to the Russians and bring them down on us?'

'That is correct. You send in Morse "SOS British submarine" and give our position.'

Jason's voice was cold. 'What makes you think I would?'

'You'll be giving the ship's company a chance, Jason. Or maybe you don't care? Maybe you don't give a tuppenny cuss if they all go, Jason?'

Jason's face was dead white. It was a fluke! A chance shot at his most vulnerable point! Why should it now affect him so deeply? He did not know. It was out of all reason ... Cubit could not possibly know ... He groaned. His neck tendons were splayed. He struggled to control himself.

'Hello . . .? Hello . . .?' Cubit was saying.

Jason could not speak. He shook, holding the phone, unable to utter a coherent phrase.

'Listen, Jason,' Cubit said. 'You've got a clock. It's now 0115 hours. We'll give you fifteen minutes. It's no good taking it, saying you've sent the message when you haven't. If nothing happens fast, we let fly with that buoy. And if you don't think that's going to bring the Russians round, we'll let out an oil slick to make sure. Fifteen minutes!'

He slammed the phone into the rack.

Jason was sitting bent forward in one of the steersman's seats in the control room. There were patches of red on his face. His eye muscle was going. He looked groggy, like a boxer who has taken a beating but is coming up for the next round.

Connor watched him anxiously from the intercom. Minute by minute, they had gained half an hour, an hour, by argument, by slanging matches with Haynes and Cubit, by making them talk – every time-consuming ruse they could think of. Men from the wardroom had caught the shouted exchanges. They were crowded at the door.

It was now 0237 hours. 'Thirty-eight minutes to go,' Connor said.

The intercom buzzed again. Jason snapped round in his seat, made a quick negative gesture. They let it buzz again.

Connor unhooked. 'Control room, Lieutenant Connor.'

'Give me Jason.' It was Cubit's voice. 'Quick!'

'What is it?' Connor said.

'Cut it out, Connor!' Cubit shouted. 'Get Jason, you bastard!'

Connor held out the phone. Jason grabbed it. 'By God, I'll have you flogged round the fleet, yet!'

'Stick it, Jason! Stick it —' Cubit was shouting. 'This is the lot! We're sending that buoy up now.'

'You damned idiot! Who's going to see it in the dark?'

'It'll be light soon enough. Now you can all go and —' Cubit rang off.

173

Jason seemed to sag. Connor was facing him. Was Jason going to crack up? Jason was obviously taking punishment. But they were both exhausted.

'Clyde, they mean it. They're going to do it.'

Simultaneously they both glanced at the clock.

'Thirty-six minutes,' Connor said. 'We've got to stop them.'

Jason's lips came back from his teeth. Connor buzzed the crew's mess. There was no answer. He jabbed the button hard again.

'Haynes,' the voice said harshly.

'This is Lieutenant Connor. Listen to me, Haynes. We can't get the signal away. Have some sense, man, if you let that buoy up, you'll be committing suicide just as surely as if you went up alone.'

Haynes put his hand over the mouthpiece. Then he came back. 'We've given you bastards time enough. I've just opened the oil valves at two and three tubes. There's going to be an oil slick half a mile long up there.'

'Haynes, listen to me —'

Jason snatched the phone from him. His face was working. He held the phone without speaking for a moment.

'Hello . . .? Hello . . .?' Haynes was saying.

Jason said, 'This is the Captain speaking. *Your Captain, Haynes*. Shut those oil valves! If any of us are going up, the oil's going to foul our escape gear, foul our lungs.'

'Look here, Jason —'

'Do as I say, damn your eyes!'

Haynes faltered. There was a break, then an exchange of voices at the other end as if they were consulting. Cubit came on in place of Haynes. 'If that signal is not going out already Jason, you've had it.'

'*Have you shut those oil valves?*'

Cubit seemed to believe he had gained the upper hand – or he sensed something else in the urgency of Jason's tone. He answered quietly, in a changed voice. 'Yes . . . we've shut 'em. What's your signal?'

Jason hesitated. 'We are now making "SOS disabled British submarine."'

'Who's the radio man?'

'Kirby.'

'What about the position?'

'We are giving the position.' Suddenly Jason bawled, 'You won't get far once we're out, Cubit. I'll settle your bloody hash!'

'Stow it! Put Kirby on,' Cubit said. 'Keep this line open and get Kirby. Don't try any tricks, Jason, or I'll personally see you get roughed-up in the Lubianka.'

Jason screwed up his eyes and shook his head. Again, Connor thought of a boxer. Open-mouthed, Jason met his look. He nodded. He was holding the intercom phone to his chest.

'But good God, you're not going to —'

'Get Kirby!'

Connor turned and went to the radio recess and signed to Kirby to come. Kirby took the earphones off and put them down. Connor shouted into the wardroom, 'Groves! Get on that set!' As Kirby turned, Groves hurried forward and took his place. They could hear Cubit's voice over the intercom: 'Kirby? You there, Kirby . . .?'

Kirby looked at Jason. Jason passed him the phone. Kirby took it, still looking inquiringly at Jason. Scarcely perceptibly, Jason nodded. His head was bent towards the earpiece. Kirby said, 'Hello, Kirby speakin'.'

'Kirby. This is Cubit. Say something. I want to get your voice.'

Kirby said, 'This is Jock Kirby speakin'. What d'you want, man, I'm waitin'?' The voice and accent were unmistakable.

'Stand there alone, Jock. Tell Jason and Connor to get away.'

Nobody moved. Kirby said, 'Aye?'

'Are you making a radio signal?'

Kirby's eyes went to Jason's. Jason nodded.

'Aye, Cubit. We're makin' a signal.'

'What are you sending, Jock?'

Kirby's look was fixed on Jason. Sweat was running down

Jason's face. Connor stood motionless, staring at Jason. Kirby swallowed.

'Quick, Kirby! Let's have it,' Cubit said.

Jason's hand touched Kirby's arm and lowered the phone. He put his lips to Kirby's ear and whispered. Kirby swallowed again and said into the phone, 'Aye, lad, I don't know why I should be tellin' you, but we're sending "SOS disabled British submarine" and givin' our position.'

'What are you sending it in?'

'What do you think? Morse, o' course.'

There was a fractional pause. Kirby still held the phone. Jason hadn't moved. As he lifted his hand indicating to Kirby to hang up, somebody jumped forward from behind them, snatched the phone from Kirby's grasp, shouting into it, 'It's a lie! It's a bloody lie! Put-up job – they're not sending anything!' It was Farrell. 'Cubit, they're having you on, lot of bloody liars – it's Farrell —'

They were on him, bearing him down. Jason wrenched the phone from him. They wrestled wildly for a moment. Then Fivesman and others intervened and Farrell was lying on the deck, his face in his arms.

The intercom phone was dangling at the end of its cord. Connor wet his lips, reached for it. Jason put out a hand and took it himself.

'Hello . . . Hello . . .' He listened, then said, 'Is that Cubit?'

Sharply, Cubit's voice said, 'That cooked your goose, didn't it, Jason?'

'Listen, you red slob, we are leaving this ship in twenty-two minutes and I hope you're not left behind.' Jason hung up, took the Tannoy broadcaster and switched on. 'Ship's company. Ship's company. Captain to ship's company. You've all stuck it out and now here's good news for you. We're going to be picked up. A submarine is moving in for us. She's already very close and as soon as she is overhead we are going to leave with the escape gear. Every man is to get his escape gear and stand by. Nobody to leave yet. Punchard, report back if you have heard this and understand. Petty Officer Fitch, report you have heard this and understand the orders.'

The men at the door shuffled and gave a ragged murmur. Jason turned. 'Get that gear ready!' Fivesman jerked Farrell to his feet and took him off.

The intercom phone buzzed. 'PO Punchard, sir. Orders received and understood, sir. Blimey, sir, it's sort of a surprise like. I mean —'

'You all right, Punchard?'

'Yes, sir.'

'Gear in order?'

'Yes, sir.'

'Then stand by.'

Connor came up. 'Trimmer's come to. He's nearly finished – but he's conscious.'

'Did he hear what I just said, about getting away?' Jason's face had changed.

'I don't know.'

'He'll never make it. It's no good trying to get him up. Will you give him another shot of morphine? If it's possible, don't let him see the others getting that escape gear out.'

'We finished the morphine last night.'

Jason looked at him aghast. 'Oh Christ . . .' He seemed to crumple.

The intercom rang. Connor let it go – but at last snatched it up. 'Control room, Lieutenant Connor.' His back was turned to Jason.

'Put Jason on, you Goddamned stooge,' Cubit's voice said.

'Say what you have to me or shut up!' Connor shouted.

'You can take your bloody lies and you know what —'

Connor cut off. He turned. Jason wasn't looking at him. 'I can't leave that man to die alone in this ship, Jack. It's – it can't be done.'

'It'll be hopeless trying to get him up.'

'But think of him – seeing everybody else go, then maybe hanging on for two hours till the charges go up. It's inhuman. *I can't do it.*'

'He's as good as finished. You're needed. You'll have to give an account of everything.'

'If I leave that poor devil I'll be dead!. I'll be dead in my soul, for God's sake! I'd rather finish it out here. I've had that, I've been through it. Not any more.'

The intercom rang again. Turning towards it, Connor bumped into Kirby. Kirby was waiting with a signal and had evidently overheard Jason. 'Time-check, sir,' he said, holding out the signal.

'Jesus,' Connor said quietly. He took it, glanced at the clock. 'Nineteen more minutes.'

The intercom was still ringing. Connor answered: 'Control room.'

'All right, Connor,' Cubit said cockily. 'We get your game. No submarine's coming in here to pick us up and you know it. All you want is to get shot of us. Up we go and get "rescued", eh? Well, we're hanging on, see? Till the Russians get here. Because the buoy's up, Connor. D'you hear? She's up there. Tell Jason he can check it. You've still got a chance to save your skins by calling the Russians and . . .'

Connor cut the communication. He took three steps to the marker-buoy control panel. His torch showed a red disc. 'They've done it,' he said over his shoulder. 'The buoy's up.'

Jason looked as if he were regaining control of himself. Connor gave him a moment more, then said, 'Clyde – the time.'

Jason's eyes went to the clock. 'Seventeen and a half more minutes. Must give the orders. Get the cipher books and log – weighted bag. On the bridge.'

As Connor turned to the ladder, he said, 'Wait! Tell Bailey to switch off the wardroom intercom. Can't have Trimmer hearing this. We can tell the others in there separately.'

Connor disappeared. Jason waited a moment, swaying with fatigue, eyes on the clock, then he switched on the Tannoy. 'Captain speaking. Captain to ship's company. Captain to ship's company. Listen carefully to these orders, all of you. The submarine *Stingray* is coming in to pick us up. She is now just over sixteen minutes away. In sixteen minutes from now we will all leave the ship wearing escape gear. I am going to give you a count-down from twenty seconds before we go. I am going to count down from twenty to zero and at zero the first men in each section go out followed by the others as fast as they can. Is that clear? When you hear my voice reach zero, out you go, double-quick. *Stingray* will be standing by overhead to pick you up. Everything depends on our carrying this out to the second. It will be barely first light. You will all have to use your eyes to spot the submarine and get to her fast. Your life may depend on your reaching the ship with utmost dispatch. Is that clear? She can't hang around up there. So get to her, hang on the casing. Try to climb up, don't wait to be dragged on board. Now take up your positions by the escape chambers. One man to stand by the intercom. Petty Officer Punchard, before you go you will set the demolition charge in the after compartment to explode two hours after we've left, that is at 0515. I repeat 0515. Report back that you have done so and any queries.'

He stood by, shaking the sweat off his face. Punchard's voice came through! 'PO Punchard. All clear, sir. We got it. No queries.'

As he cut off, Cubit's voice came raucously up on the Tannoy. Cubit had abandoned the intercom phone and was using the Tannoy mike in the mess, trying to drown out Jason.

'You think you're going to panic us with that stuff, Jason? You — liars, you warmongering bastards, the lot of you! The mad wolves don't take us in. The mighty forces of the Soviet Union are going to defeat you – put all you western fascist hyenas where you belong! The mighty people of the Soviet Union are —'

'Petty Officer Fitch! Petty Officer Robertson,' Jason was shouting him down, his face thrust out, straining at the Tannoy, crouching like a man with a wild animal on his back. He was managing to cover Cubit's voice. 'Bosco! All of you – all of you in that mess. I beg you to save yourselves. Get into your gear. Fitch! Robertson! Do you hear me? Get up to the chamber. I appeal to you in the name of the service, in the name of your families. This is your last chance to escape . . .

We have only fourteen minutes. Robertson, do you hear this . . .?'

Connor reached the bottom of the ladder and stopped at the sight of Jason. Jason, pleading with the men, wasn't cracking up. He was being torn apart. Connor dumped the cipher bag and turned away. Groves was at the receiver in the radio recess. He went into the wardroom.

The dimly lit space was full of sweating half-naked men fitting on their escape gear. He pushed in among them. Bailey and Fivesman were supervising them, explaining, pulling straps, adjusting mouthpieces. Connor gave Bailey and Fivesman the orders to pass on to the men. He noticed Kirby quickly get up from Trimmer's side and come for the door.

'Relieve Groves at the set, Kirby.'

'Aye, aye, sir. Just goin'.' Kirby had his escape gear. He shot Connor a curious look. Connor pressed in among the men. It was impossible in the restricted space to prevent Trimmer seeing the preparations for escape. Trimmer's eyes were open. He was lying on his back on the long seat behind the table with his head turned watching the others fit their gear. His expression seemed to have cleared. He understood.

Connor took a grip on himself. He could not leave Jason the task of explaining. He tugged at the straps of one of the men's gear to defer the moment. Then he went over to Trimmer.

Those near edged away, turned their backs. They talked in lower voices.

Connor squatted at Trimmer's side.

'How goes it, Trimmer?'

'Not so dusty, sir.'

'Comfortable?'

A nod.

'Do you want a drink?'

'No thanks.'

'We'll get you another pill in a minute.'

The appalling difficulty of communication, of being able to offer no hope, settled on Connor. He squatted there while the men moved about round them. He tried to lie. 'This is an exercise, you see, Trimmer. Have to be ready. After all, we

180

haven't had one since we landed down here.'

Trimmer said, 'It's all right, sir.' He had the glimmer of a smile. There was another pause. Trimmer said, 'You'd better get your gear, sir.'

'All right, Trimmer.' Connor got up. He felt a coward. He hadn't been able to tell Trimmer. 'I'll be back.' He pushed his way through the men to the control room.

Jason was still bent at the Tannoy, pleading with the eight in the mess, face haggard, dripping sweat. '. . . on my honour as a naval officer, do you hear? On my honour as a naval officer, I swear to you that is the truth. The ship is going to be blown up two hours after we have left. You can't stop it. You cannot control the demolition charges from your section. We are all leaving in six minutes from now. Six minutes . . . do you hear?'

'Clyde,' Connor took his arm. 'Leave them. You can't do any more.'

As Jason swung round to face him, Cubit's voice cut in.

'Go to bloody hell, Jason.'

Connor snatched the mike from Jason's hand and hooked it up. Jason was crouching and battered with defeat. He didn't seem to see Connor for a moment; then he said, 'They won't listen. They say I'm lying. I can't get it over to them.'

'Then let them go to hell!'

Jason focused. 'What about Trimmer?'

'He's in there. He knows what's going on.'

Like a dazed man, Jason went slowly to the door of the wardroom. Connor turned and watched him. At the door he saw Jason stiffen and quickly stepped up behind him.

'Good Christ, Trimmer. What are you doing?'

Trimmer was propped up against the bulkhead and Kirby and Lockwood were helping him into his escape gear. Jason went forward. 'What's this, Trimmer? Who moved him, Kirby? You know damned well —'

'We're all going out, ain't we, sir?' Trimmer said. 'That was the orders. Think I'm going to stay behind on me own, playin' gin rummy?' He slipped. Kirby and Lockwood grabbed him.

181

For one moment Jason stood staring at him. Then he said, 'All right, Trimmer. By God, we'll get you out.'

'Three more minutes, sir,' Connor said. 'Here's your gear.'

Jason took it. 'I am going to broadcast the count-down. Get up into the fin, up to the chamber, all of you.'

CHAPTER FIFTEEN

IN THE GENERAL darkness of the sky and the sea, the Submarine *Stingray* was visible only as a faint white outline on the surface where the sea washed against her casing. A dozen lookouts on the catwalk fore and aft of the conning-tower were scanning the water. Above them, Lieutenant-Commander Whitfield, the commanding officer, Lieutenant Ferris, his No. 1, and Lane, the Yeoman of Signals, were together on the open bridge of the conning tower.

The first greying of dawn was appearing in the sky over *Stingray*'s starboard bow. The air was fresh. There was a small lop on. A light spray blew from the bow wave. None of the men was speaking. Apart from the hiss of the sea and the throb of the diesels, the only sound was the gabble from the voice-pipe giving the time at twenty-second intervals.

'Oh three one four hours.'

The Yeoman was checking the times by the luminous dial of his watch. Whitfield and Ferris had their forearms resting on the conning-tower casing, looking out over the sea. Whitfield bent to the voice-pipe and spoke to the control room. 'What's the set now?'

'Six and a half knots, sir. It's falling off a bit, sir.'

'Group down, dead slow together.'

'Group down, dead slow together, sir.' The telegraph rang.

The grey area of sky had spread and become more luminous.

'Can't see anything, sir,' Ferris said.

'Get a bearing?'

'Not yet, sir.'

Whitfield spoke into the voice-pipe again. 'Anything firm on sonar yet?'

'No, sir. We're still getting a lot of blur. Looks like some throw-off trick. Could be shore defences.'

Whitfield turned his glasses towards the shore. It was still masked by mist or rain. But the mist would lift as soon as the sun was up.

'Oh three one five,' the voice-pipe said.

Whitfield snatched up a megaphone – they dared not use the R/T – and leaned forward to the lookouts. 'Lookouts for'ard. They're coming up. Watch out.'

Below, in *Uranus*, Jason's voice was repeating the escape count over the Tannoy. 'Zero, zero. This is zero. Every man to leave the ship. This is zero. Zero. Every man out of the ship. Zero . . . zero . . .'

One by one, from the different sections of the ship, the men began to go out through the escape chambers – Monkhouse, Hoyle, Evans, Trimmer, Kirby first from the control room; Maxwell, Davis, Beale from the engine room. Punchard and Bailey were supervising the exits. Under the ladder to the torpedo-room escape chamber, Robertson was bending over Wingrove, fitting his gear.

'Zero. This is zero . . .'

'You're a dirty bleeding liar, Jason,' Cubit shouted into the mike. His body was gleaming with sweat. In this section as well, the men had begun to go. Their temporary allegiance to Cubit and Haynes had begun to break down under Jason's long harangue over the Tannoy. Savage and Green were out. Cubit had shouted his contempt at them. Now Fitch and Bosco had strapped on their gear but still held the breathing-masks to their chests, looking doubtfully at Cubit.

'Petty Officer Fitch, do you hear me? Everybody is leaving. Do you hear me?'

'The Russians'll take your balls off, Jason!'

'Fitch! Robertson! Get that bloody Commie out of the way. Answer me! I'm leaving in one minute.'

Fitch made a move towards the torpedo room. 'Maybe it's right after all, Cubit.'

'Go on, you pair of bastards!' Cubit's face was contorted with scorn. 'Your master's cracking the whip!'

Fitch turned towards the torpedo room, pulling the mask on

184

over his head. Bosco followed him.

'Scum of the imperialist warmongers!'

In the rising light, the men of *Stingray*'s casing party were becoming individualized. They held lines ready to throw to survivors and had scrambling nets over the side.

Whitfield had swung round and was repeating the call to the lookouts aft. 'Watch out! Yell as soon as you see them.'

'Looks like a squall red five oh, sir,' the Yeoman said.

It was poor visibility.

'Oh three one five forty seconds ... Oh three one six,' the voice-pipe said.

'Light bearing green eight oh, sir,' the Yeoman said.

Whitfield had already fixed it with his glasses. It was the first light he had glimpsed from the direction of the shore. He watched anxiously but the light did not appear to be moving. Then it disappeared as the rain or mist intervened again.

'Oh three one six, twenty seconds ... Oh three one six forty ...'

'Can't see 'em, sir,' Ferris said.

Oh Christ, we've missed them, Whitfield was saying to himself. I think we've missed them.

'Do you hear me?' Jason's voice seemed to fill the mess. 'For the last time, I am telling you to leave for the last time.'

Haynes was leaning against the bulkhead intently watching Cubit. His lips were open and teeth clenched.

'Captain to torpedo room. This is the last minute you can save yourselves. I am leaving the ship.'

Neither of the two moved.

'Cubit?' Jason's voice said out of the silence. 'Cubit, are you still there?'

Cubit let a few seconds go by. He was breathing through his mouth. 'Sure, I'm here, Jason.' He dropped the mike away from his mouth for a second. His voice was a whisper. 'And I'm going to keep you with me.'

'Who's there in the compartment with you?'

'Why, we're all here, Jason.' He turned his head as if speak-

185

ing to somebody beside him. 'Ain't we, Robbie?'

They could hear Jason's breathing close to the mike at the other end and the demolition control bell ringing in the control room.

'Cubit, you're a liar.'

'You'd like to think so, wouldn't you?'

'You're a bloody liar!'

'You're wrong, Jason. This is where I win.'

'You're a bloody Communist bastard!'

'This is where I'm somebody. We're reversing the roles, Jason. That's what it's all about, eh? One side reversing the roles on the other. Your world's through, Jason, and ours is taking over.'

'Tell me the truth!'

'It's taking over everywhere – Africa, Asia, in the Americas —'

'Can't you tell me the truth, Cubit?' Suddenly Jason's voice was pathetically pleading. 'Have they gone?'

'– and there's no place in it for you, Jason. Your class won't have any more commanding to do. You're going to be squashed like filthy parasites —'

'Cubit, those men can't be with you! I ask you to tell me the truth!'

'– and your children are going to knuckle down to the dictatorship of the toiling masses.'

'How many have gone?' Now Jason was shouting at the top of his voice. 'Who's there? Fitch? Savage? Robertson?'

'It's the end of you, Jason! We're all here. We all think the same. The Russians'll be here for us in half an hour and we'll get you and that bloody submarine, and your bloody warmongering government. You're through, you're finished . . .'

A reddish tinge was invading the horizon. But dawn seemed to be diffusing the light, thickening it into milky opacity which at one moment closed to within a few hundred yards of *Stingray* and the next was treacherously shifting.

'Oh three one seven . . .'

'Where in God are they?' Whitfield said.

186

'Can't see anything in this.'

'Aircraft, sir,' the Yeoman said. They had all heard the sound of several planes overhead. Nothing was visible. They listened as the sound approached and passed seaward.

'Dawn patrol,' Ferris said. 'Seem high up.' Then from shoreward another aircraft was approaching, a straggler trying to catch the others. It was flying distinctly lower, a piston engine.

'Here it comes, green fifty.' They glimpsed the long grey shape between the clouds. With interminable slowness the aircraft passed over. They stood waiting for the sound of the turn which would indicate a sighting. But the hum faded to seaward.

'Oh three one eight, twenty.'

It was generally much lighter.

'Oh three one eight, forty.'

Whitfield lifted the megaphone and called to the men forward. 'Can't you see anything, there?'

One or two turned, shook their heads.

'Lights bearing green thirty and seventy, sir,' the Yeoman said. 'More dead ahead, sir.'

The shore had abruptly become visible. They could see strings of lights paling in the gaining daylight.

'We can't keep this up,' Whitfield said anxiously.

Wingrove was leaning in the doorway of the torpedo room with the goggled mask of the escape gear on his chest. Cubit had seen him as soon as he had appeared. Slowly Wingrove moved forward. Cubit's hand flicked open the razor. He extended his arm; then his eye caught the glint of the valve spanner which Wingrove held at his side.

Wingrove put out his free hand.

Cubit tossed him the mike, watching Wingrove's face.

'Captain, sir. Torpedo room calling Captain. Captain sir, Wingrove speaking . . .'

Suddenly and with urgent hope, Jason's voice said, 'Who is it?'

'Wingrove, sir. Only Cubit, Haynes and me left, sir. All the

187

rest have gone. We're leaving now.'

'Thank you, Wingrove. Get out – quick!'

'Good luck, sir.' Wingrove hung up.

They stood looking at each other. The scrubber had faded completely. There was no sound except their breathing. 'Want to go?' Wingrove said.

Haynes looked from Wingrove to Cubit. He wet his lips.

The ghost of a smile came to Wingrove's face. 'Sure – now we're all going out together. Ain't we, Cubit?'

Lieutenant Ferris had his glasses to his eyes. 'Something moving over the shore there. I wouldn't mind betting that's the airfield and they've got a helicopter up.'

A fresh voice broke in on the control-room voice-pipe. 'Sonar contact dead ahead, sir. Five hundred yards. Stationary, sir. Depth two-seventy feet.'

'That's her, by God! A touch half ahead. Keep that contact. Can't you see anything down there?'

'A touch half ahead, sir.'

Ferris still had the glasses to his eyes. 'Don't like the look of that helicopter.'

'No sign of any survivors, sir,' the Yeoman said. 'The contact might be wreck or defences, sir.'

Whitfield shot him a look. He shouted down the voice-pipe: 'Could that contact be shore defences?'

'Firm contact, seems pretty sizeable, sir. We are closing.'

'Helicopter looks as if it's moving seaward, sir,' Ferris said.

The northern daylight was now spreading over the whole area. They could clearly see the low coastline, the towers of the shore installation, the clusters of buildings.

'We shall have to dive,' Whitfield said. 'Get those men in, Yeoman. Diving stations. Keep the sonar contact. Close up torpedo stations.'

'Hold on, sir. Something dead ahead.' The Yeoman's voice was excited.

'What the hell. Keep your stations!'

They strained forward, looking at the grey water.

'Port five.'

'Port five, sir.'

'What in Christ is it?'

The minutes were interminable as the submarine moved forward.

'Looks like a buoy, sir.'

'Good God – a marker buoy. Stop both.'

'Stop both, sir.'

'Man to port, sir!' The shout came up from below.

'Two men to starboard, sir.'

In a moment, all the lookouts were shouting that they had spotted survivors in the water. The heads of swimming men in goggled breathing-gear had suddenly appeared in the sea on both sides. They looked very small. The lookouts were throwing their lines, scrambling down the nets to grab the men.

'More of 'em hanging on to the buoy, sir.'

Through the megaphone Whitfield yelled to the foremost lookouts to secure a line to the buoy as the submarine came slowly up.

'What's that bloody helicopter doing?'

'Can't see for the moment, sir.'

'Pull those men aboard for the love of God! Chief, get rid of that buoy. Unship it or sink the bloody thing.'

'Helicopter seems to be coming out, sir.'

'Hell's bloody bells, *move* there, all of you!'

Hunched and shivering in blankets and borrowed clothes, they stood crowded in *Stingray*'s wardroom and the surrounding spaces, childishly talkative with relief. The ship was under way at speed and vibrating. Fivesman had ticked off the names on the list. There were six missing: Trimmer, Acre, Davis, Wingrove, Cubit and Haynes.

'I saw Cubit and Wingrove together a minute, sir,' Punchard said. 'When I looked again, they were gone, both of 'em.'

Robertson said, 'I couldn't get Wingrove to come up with me. There was something he wanted to make sure of.'

Jason looked round their cold, wet, unshaved English seamen's faces. He said, 'Yes. I know.'

THE WORLD'S GREATEST THRILLER WRITERS – NOW AVAILABLE IN GRANADA PAPERBACKS

Len Deighton

Twinkle, Twinkle, Little Spy	85p	☐
Yesterday's Spy	95p	☐
Spy Story	85p	☐
Horse Under Water	95p	☐
Billion Dollar Brain	95p	☐
The Ipcress File	95p	☐
An Expensive Place to Die	95p	☐
Declarations of War	95p	☐
Bomber	£1.25	☐
The Best of Len Deighton Gift Set	£5.95	☐

Peter Van Greenaway

Doppelganger	60p	☐
The Medusa Touch	85p	☐
Take the War to Washington	75p	☐
Judas!	75p	☐
Suffer! Little Children	95p	☐

Ted Allbeury

Snowball	95p	☐
A Choice of Enemies	95p	☐
Palomino Blonde	95p	☐
The Special Collection	60p	☐
The Only Good German	85p	☐
Moscow Quadrille	75p	☐
The Man with the President's Mind	85p	☐

THE WORLD'S GREATEST THRILLER WRITERS – NOW AVAILABLE IN GRANADA PAPERBACKS

Robert Ludlum

The Chancellor Manuscript	£1.25 ☐
The Gemini Contenders	£1.25 ☐
The Rhinemann Exchange	£1.00 ☐
The Matlock Paper	£1.25 ☐
The Osterman Weekend	95p ☐
The Scarlatti Inheritance	95p ☐
Ludlum Super-Thrillers Gift Set	£5.95 ☐

Ian Fleming

Dr No	95p ☐
From Russia, with Love	95p ☐
Diamonds are Forever	95p ☐
On Her Majesty's Secret Service	95p ☐
Goldfinger	85p ☐
You Only Live Twice	75p ☐
Live and Let Die	75p ☐
The Man with the Golden Gun	75p ☐
Octopussy	75p ☐
Casino Royale	75p ☐
Thunderball	75p ☐